TALL SEWER

TALL SEWER

* * *

ISBN: 979-8-9916616-0-7

Front cover artwork by Andrew Vickery
Sewer illustration by Colin Terrence Lee

Grift Rocket
www.GriftRocket.com

TALL SEWER

Contents

Million Dollar Question	1
DiCaprio 1997	12
Allegory of the Cave Pt. II	18
Washington 2018	31
Movie / TV Ideas	38
Pitt 2013	51
8th Street	54
Cole 2003	99
Scraps	102
Witherspoon 2014	161
Sports	162
Hanks 1994	173
Hayek 1999	179
7th Grade Diary	189
Leguizamo 2022	203
McKinnon 2024	208
Nightmares	209
Smith 2021	247
Whitaker 2006	252
Comics	253
Reynolds 2016	255
More Scraps	263
Cut	323

MILLION DOLLAR QUESTION

I am so close to one million dollars.
So close.

I'm not a psychic, but I have lived long enough to glimpse into my own blurry future. It's bleak.

I suck at making money. My first year out of college, I was making minimum wage and didn't even know it. I thought minimum wage was what you get paid at Mc-Donald's, but no. You can actually wear pants and a shirt with buttons to work and still get paid minimum wage. It turns out that businesses enjoy paying you as little as possible. It's easier for them to make money that way. Hard to argue with the raw figures.

I got a raise after a year because "it would have been illegal not to." The accountant called me in to her office to tell me the good news and set off one of those New Years confetti poppers. I had to clean it up after. Content with this small improvement, I went to sleep and woke up five years later in the same place.

Whoops.

If I could go back and tell myself not to answer phones and make coffee for $550 a week for six years I would, but as far as I know you can't do that. One time on shrooms I thought I was sending vibrations to my past self through a puddle, but that's as close as I've ever gotten to fixing my life.

Until now.

If I don't make this million right here, I don't think I ever will. I do believe in myself—it's important to do that—but it's more important to be realistic. I will probably continue to make more money, but the way things are going (bad), I am not going to be making a million anytime soon or anytime far away.

It's just very hard to make that much money. Some guys will do something easy like invent a product or use the stock market, but for the rest of us, it's not happening.

I suppose I could start selling sandwiches for $5. Then I'd only have to sell 200,000 of them. It would probably cost money to make the sandwiches though so that would set me back a bit. I'm not very good at cooking either so this doesn't seem like a great plan for me. Just spitballing.

I've done the research and it took most rich people a long time to become rich. At least a year and sometimes much more than that. Lots of long nights at the office is what it takes. I don't like spending long nights at the office. I don't like spending long *days* at the office. The office is a place I do not like to be. Most of my time there is spent thinking about going home to smoke weed or jack off or smoke weed and jack off. Sometimes I will bat my shit around during the car ride home just so when I walk in I'm on 100 ready to go.

I don't have the patience or skill to make a lot of money over a long period of time, but I have an opportunity to make a lot of money in a very short amount of time.

And I have to take it.

I just need one person to help me. I wish I could do it alone, but I can't. Not without her. I thought about texting, but I pulled up our conversation and the last thing I sent was "happy Birthday" four months ago. The last thing she texted me was "Happy Birthday!!" seven months ago. I don't think a text conversation should define our relationship, but it is clear that I am not that close with my sister.

That's why it's eight o'clock and I'm standing on the steps to her apartment trying to figure out how I'm going to phrase this. How I'm going to knock on her door and tell my sister about the million dollar offer. How I'm going to tell my sister that if we have sex someone will give us one million dollars and my greatest fear is that she thinks I would do it for free.

My sister is two years younger than me, she's shorter than me, and she might have bangs. You might say this is a poor description of a person, but I would say this is concrete evidence that I'm not attracted to her. If I really did like her, I would be able to describe her better. But I can't. She's just another girl. I don't even know what her feet look like. Not that it would matter, but I don't. Another instance of objective proof that I don't want to fuck my

3

sister, but I doubt she would agree.

My sister is smarter than me. Way smarter. She's not a genius or anything, but I am a little dumb and she is not dumb at all. She graduated from a smart college, and I didn't. She went to medical school, and I didn't. She has hurt herself by accident much less than I have. She's not an easy person to trick. I wasn't planning on tricking her into fucking me, but if I was it probably wouldn't work. Waste of energy to even think about it.

My sister will make a million dollars. She's still in school, but it's medical school. She'll graduate and be a doctor and someone will pay her a million dollars just to do her job. She'll be set for life. She won't even have to do reluctant incest. If only we could all be so lucky.

My sister does not need the money as much as I do, and I don't even need the money. This is the real problem. I bet if I was riddled with debt, and the bill collectors were calling, and Russian men were breaking my legs, she would fuck me then. If I was really in a life or death situation and we had exhausted all possible options and the doomsday clock was ticking down to seconds and this was the only way to save my life I am 91% sure my sister would have sex with me. I know I would do the same for her. We're family, after all.

But there are no bags over my head. No one is breaking my legs. The only time I don't pay my credit card bill is when I forget to. I want this money for selfish reasons. I want a computer that is zero years old instead of seven. I want the weed they put on the top shelf. I want to take some time off work and travel Europe or chill and stay at

4

home and just kick it. I want a cheat code to skip the 30 years behind the desk that I am staring at. My sister does not want to skip anything. She is exactly where she wants to be.

My sister loves me. I don't think she likes me, but she definitely loves me. We don't hang out or text or talk, but that's just life. She's busy helping people and I have got some things going on as well. You don't have to be best friends to love each other.

We may not actually be close, but we're close the way family is close. The day Grandma died, she cried so much. I only cried a little. Mom had us when she was young, so our grandparents practically raised us. At the funeral, she put her arm around me and kept it there the whole time. I was strong for her. I kept her safe. She held me so tight. That must have meant something to her. This is the least she can do for me.

What even constitutes sex, really? Is there a time limit that needs to be surpassed? That doesn't seem fair because what if I was a premature buster? I'm not, but if someone nuts in less than 10 seconds that must still count as sex. It wouldn't be fair otherwise. I understand how it might be deemed a bit of a con if I did a quick in and out with no cum. That could be viewed as cheating, and I intend to follow the rules.

As long as I finish, that has to count as sex. I think most juries would back me up on this. Obviously I'm going to be in a bit of a bind if she has to climax too. I don't think she'd let me help with that—and even if she did, I wouldn't be much help anyway. It seems fair to assume that just one of us getting there would count. Have to remember to ask about this.

The best strategy would be to seclude myself in a room and jack off 98% of the way. Then, **blindfolded**, I enter a second room where my sister is also blindfolded, wearing noise canceling headphones, and bent over a bed. I walk forward, enter her, and finish in the most robotically efficient way possible. If my preparation is done correctly I estimate I wouldn't need more than 20 seconds (maximum) inside her to finish.

Time is our enemy here. For both of our sakes I have to minimize the total duration of the event. To ensure we hit this 20 second benchmark, I will have to forego a condom. I want to do this safely (I'm clean and I assume my sister is too), but a rubber is only going to be a setback.

Obviously if there's no condom, I'm pulling out too. I don't even think I need to say that, it's just a given. I'll take a step back and spill on the floor or something. Keep it as far away from her body as possible. Don't need anyone stepping in it.

I then exit the room, we both remove our blindfolds, and try to forget what just happened which shouldn't be too hard because barely anything happened, and we have a million dollars now.

If she wanted, she could be drunk or sedated to help fog up her memory, but I would have to be sober (don't need any substances prolonging the experience).

This is a perfect plan and she'd have to be an idiot to say no to it. This is an *Ocean's Eleven* type plan. If Danny

Ocean had to fuck his sister in one of those movies to steal a diamond or something, this is how he would do it.

I'm a little nervous if I propose this she will think I am even weirder than if we just had regular sex. Women hate when you solve problems and she might get angry if I am too good at having the most platonic incest possible. She might rather I fuck her stupid like a normal person.

If she says yes I'll submit my proposal but let her hammer out the details. That seems fair. After all, she's the one getting fucked.

This is really just a favor. A large favor. There's nothing sexual about it. I never ask her for anything so to be honest, I'm due. Last winter when she was home for Christmas I paid for movie tickets and she said she would Venmo, but she didn't. I let that go. I'm not saying the two are equal, but I've built up some goodwill over the years.

It's just like asking someone to help you move. I know she would rather not help me move, who wants to help someone move, it sucks helping someone move, but I really need to move and most good friends would help you move if you need it. I've never asked her to help me move before either. I could see if I was moving every other month she could get tired of me asking her to help move, but this is my first move. My first and only move. I'm not going to ask her to help me move again after this. It's a one time move. She has to understand that. Just one fuck and it's barely a fuck at all. I'm asking for like a quarter fuck.

I hope her boyfriend isn't here. Convincing her will be one thing, but I don't think he'll come around to this idea at all. I've never had a real girlfriend, but I imagine if I did and she said she was going to fuck her brother for money, I would be displeased. I guess it depends on the amount of money, though. A million is a lot. Feelings become much less important when a million gets involved.

They don't live together, but the way she talks about him makes it seem like he's here a lot. They've been dating for two years, I think. Maybe more. Shit, maybe they do live together. I kinda remember her talking about something big with him. Maybe he moved in or he had to stay here because of a bug thing? I really hope he's not here. I need to pay more attention to stuff my sister says. If she agrees to fuck me, I promise I will listen to her better.

If he is here, I'll have to come back another time. We get along fine—or we have, the couple of times we've met— but not well enough for him to be cool with me fucking his girlfriend who is also my sister. Even if he wasn't dating her, he probably wouldn't want me to fuck my sister...it's not like a *personal* thing.

It would be ideal if he didn't find out about this at all. We have a nice thing going where we talk about video games, and I bet he would stop these pleasantries if he finds out I'm trying to fuck his girlfriend. He doesn't seem like the jealous type, but... you know.

Well.

KNOCK KNOCK KNOCK

• • • • •

When I was in the fifth grade, I took a test called the ERB. It's the SAT for middle schoolers. Designed to test reading, writing, and basic mathematic skills, but more importantly, it's exposure to standardized testing. Teaching kids how to deal with pressure. Preparation. Filling in the little bubbles.

I was so nervous before the test I barely slept. If the SAT determined what college you went to then this test would surely have equal consequences. Ten year olds are not supposed to feel this much stress. I didn't have enough gray matter to handle it. The proctor told us we had 35 minutes. Pencils down when the clock hits 10:05.

I opened the test packet, took a deep breath, and freaked out. There was no way I could do this in 35 minutes. I started moving so fast I was doing math without checking, skipping lines for reading comprehension, and just guessing on vocab. Even if I got some wrong at least I would finish. There's no way the test would judge me as "stupid" as long as I managed to finish.

At the 35th minute I put my pencil down. The proctor told us to take a drink of water. The next section would start in five minutes.

The next section.

The next section.

The next section.

I thought it was all one section. I tried to do the whole three hour test in 35 minutes.

I spent the next two and a half hours frantically erasing every answer and trying to work my way back. Ironically, having more time made me even more stressed. I knew I'd completely blown the first section and proceeded to fuck up the rest.

By the actual end, my paper was so fucked from my eraser marks that the Scantron couldn't read it. I had to admit I didn't understand the rules and take the test again with the slow kids who need extra time.

I still think about that sick feeling. Realizing how badly I didn't understand what was asked of me. How I let my nerves get the best of me. How if I had just asked one question I could have avoided all of it.

I thought this was the biggest fuck up of my life until yesterday when I told my sister that someone would pay us a million dollars if we fucked, fucked her, and then didn't get paid a million dollars.

It's not like I lost a best friend, but she doesn't wish me happy birthday anymore. The few times a year we're in the same room she will do her best to exit that room. I know she doesn't believe me. Thinks I was lying about the whole thing. She says I raped her. Jesus Christ. Does she know how that makes me feel? She agreed to it! I just got some of the finer details wrong. Obviously things didn't work out the way we wanted them to, but we can at least be adults about this.

There's no amount of proof I can show her that the offer was real. At this point, even if there was I doubt she would care. I just didn't understand the rules. Didn't ask enough questions. That's on me. I'll deal with it.

I thought she was my only sibling. I didn't know Mom was pregnant. I didn't know my Mom *could get* pregnant.

At least now I know there's no time limit. The million is still on the table. It never left. We can do this whenever and get paid. I'm no freak either. I have a code. Morals. I can wait. I would never do something that she can't consent to.

She's going to be born in May. I waited this long. I can answer phones for a bit longer.

I've got a very important question to ask my new sister on her 18th birthday.

1997 PRESS JUNKET - LEONARDO DICAPRIO

INTERVIEWER: Thanks for sitting down with us today, Leo.

LEONARDO DICAPRIO: No problem, no problem. Happy to sit. I love New York.

INT: *Titanic*. Wow. So exciting. Was the ship really that big? It looks pretty big!

DICAPRIO: You know what I love most about New York? The trains. I love how the trains run you know? Cuz me and Tobey—oh my god—me and Tobey always run train, haha. So much tag team shit, we're some real sickos when we wanna be.

INT: Wow.

DICAPRIO: Yeah, so funny story. You know how in social groups—guy groups, girl groups—doesn't matter. There's always an alpha. That's kind of an overused word—like a queen bee. That's kind of gay actually. Not like the leader, but there is someone who has the most... I don't know, suction, standing, whatever you want to call it. When you're getting into a car there's a guy who's getting shot-gun and a guy who's riding bitch. When you're sitting down at dinner there's a guy who sits in the center of the table and a guy who gets stranded at the end. When you go to a movie with two other people, someone has to sit in the middle, right? And the thing about it is, for this guy he's not even like engineering the situation to get to these spots. It just happens for him. And then the real thing about it is, the people around him aren't even consciously giving him these positions. Everyone is in lockstep to give one guy the best seat, the best table, the best life. And they don't even notice it.

INT: And you're that guy?

DICAPRIO: Yeah, I'm fucking Leonardo DiCaprio of course I'm that guy. But I'm not a dick about it. Obviously this happens to me, but there's a way to play it cool. I give up the good seat sometimes, but never more than I take it. I'm getting off base—listen. So yeah, I'm *the guy*. And—I love him to death, one of my best friends—but Tobey is not the guy. That's just the truth. And I don't think there is a clearer real world example of this then when we tag team sluts.

INT: Sluts?

DICAPRIO: Groupies, sluts, slizz, whatever you want to call them, but they're sure as hell not *girls*. Girls don't let us do what we do to them. [Leo laughs] So when me and Tobey got something going in a hotel or wherever usually there's a moment when the thing goes to the bathroom and we huddle. I look Tobey in the eye and we know it's on. I don't gotta say shit, but what I am saying is, "I'm taking the pussy and you're getting the mouth."

INT: It's kind of an understood agreement then? You split it up before?

DICAPRIO: Yeah, we [Leo raises his hands to do air quotes] "split it up." But I *always* get the pussy and Tobey always gets the mouth. I don't switch. I never switch.

INT: Is that a fair split? I wouldn't know.

DICAPRIO: [Leo cracks up laughing] No, no it's not a fair split. First of all it's way easier to nut off pussy. Just feels better. Second, you can really control the rhythm back there. Hands on the hips, you got something to hold on to, you can actually fuck you know? But the guy getting mouth is totally at your mercy. When you're really drilling that shit you're basically controlling the rhythm that her mouth hits your boy's cock. Honestly, it's kind of gay for the other guy. I'm more in charge of how his dick is getting sucked than the girl is. Her body is just a conduit for the power I'm throwing down back there. This one time I was fuuuucked. Like crazy fucked up and I was fucking so hard man I sent the chick into Tobey so fast he fell backwards off the bed and slammed his head on the nightstand.

INT: So, Tobey is not your friend?

DICAPRIO: What? No, he's like my best friend. Listen. It goes back to what I was saying earlier. In our friendship

I am always sitting shotgun. I am always getting the bigger slice. I am always getting the pussy while he gets the leftovers. It's just the way relationships work. It's never a perfect 50/50 split. You might just blow up a friendship if you look too deep and realize you're the guy always getting shafted.

INT: What was it like filming with all the water on *Titanic*? Were you scared?

DICAPRIO: At least that's what I *thought* until a few days ago. So me and Tobey are ripping this thing up. But I'm crazy drunk. Like way more fucked up than usual and I can already tell I'm not gonna cum. I'm doing my best, but I just can't get over the hill. I'm losing interest. So I kind of phase out and look up at Tobey and you know what I see? This guy has the biggest smile on his face. He's loving this shit. We've done this hundreds of times, maybe thousands, and he's fucking her face like it's his first time ever getting his dick wet.

INT: He was enjoying himself it sounds like.

DICAPRIO: Fucking A, right? It had me thinking, does Tobey *actually like* getting head more than pussy? It sure looks like he does! I thought I was being selfish, hogging all the good hole, but this guy might actually like the smaller slice more. So maybe that's why these friendships work. Some guys, it ruins their whole fucking day if they're in the backseat. Huffing and puffing, counting down the seconds til they get out of the car. But there are some guys that are fine with having their knees up to their chest riding bitch. They like it somehow. That's how all this works. How the world works. How society functions. Some people naturally want less. They're content with it. And maybe I'm missing something in life because I always want more. I don't know.

INT: What was Kate Winslet like on set? Any real life chemistry there?

DICAPRIO: I wish I drowned for real. That would have made everything easier.

6 Things to Tell Your Co-Workers After They Catch You Eating Sand

1. That was rice

2. What did you say? I didn't hear you.

3. That was brown rice.

4. That wasn't sand you saw me eating.

5. That was another guy you saw eating sand. Not me.

6. It's good for you to eat sand. It's healthy.

THE ALLEGORY OF THE CAVE PT. II

Translation by Willard F. Snow

PART ONE:
SETTING THE SCENE:
THE ARIST AND THE AUDIENCE

SOCRATES: Imagine this: A man raises paint to parchment, purpose to papyrus. He is an artist. He carries his tools (paint, brush, easel) to the park and through it. He scouts a subject, lit by the noonish sun, and begins.

A fire rages above and inside him.

SOCRATES: His start is immediate. Before second thoughts can form, before first thoughts can form, the artist begins. Like the well he *lowers* a bucket into himself, retrieves what he can, and puts it on the page. His process is a permanent state of being. No man nor monsoon could stop him now.

Spectators draw and a crowd forms.

SOCRATES: Through no intent of his own, a show has started. What began as a personal pursuit has blossomed into a public performance. A ring develops around him and another ring after that. Concentric circles form until the very theatre of Epidaurus has been reconstructed. Alone in the epicenter the artist continues to work.

GLAUCON: How many men watch the artist?

SOCRATES: The highest number imaginable.

GLAUCON: 1,000?

SOCRATES: Yes.

The Sun travels and the crowd wanes.

SOCRATES: The vice grip that once held their attention loosens. 2,000 eyes turn to 200, turn to 20, turn to 2.
But despite the fading attention, the artist does not lose pace. His drive is not tied to applause nor praise. It is tethered to nothing. He began alone and alone he shall end.

Two eyes remain.

SOCRATES: The artist relaxes his shoulders. He lowers his hand. Paint drips down the canvas and back to earth. One spectator lingers. A woman. She allows a moment of silence for the artist to bask in his piece. She speaks:

WOMAN: This looks like shit.

PART TWO:
THE DIALOGUE

WOMAN: It doesn't look very good.

ARTIST: Hmmm.

WOMAN: Like a child's drawing. It looks like a child made this.

ARTIST: I made this. And I'm not a child.

WOMAN: I didn't say you were. But based on the quality of the work it looks like a child made this. I know you made it because I watched you make it and I also know you are not a child for similar reasons. But it's bad and it looks like a kid made it.

ARTIST: I made it look like this on purpose.

WOMAN: I don't believe you.

ARTIST: It's the truth.

WOMAN: You looked like you were working hard on it for a long time.

ARTIST: I was.

WOMAN: But the painting does not reflect that. You tried hard and the painting looks bad.

ARTIST: I was trying hard to make it look bad. I—

WOMAN: No—

ARTIST: —I succeeded.

WOMAN: I don't believe you.

ARTIST: It's the truth.

WOMAN: Ok.

ARTIST: It is.

WOMAN: *lowers eyes*

ARTIST: Let me explain.

ARTIST: The other day I was walking to buy cigarettes and if there was a hotdog on the roller I would probably buy that too, but I was mostly walking to get cigarettes. I'm walking and I pass an elementary school with these huge windows. It's Saturday so there are no kids there, but the windows are still there.

I stop at the window and in the center it says, "React Against Corporate Tobacco," and then wallpapered all around it are dozens of kid's drawings. Pictures of smoky lungs, cigarettes with big red cancel signs over them, parents smoking while their kids cry, stuff like that. There are a lot of ideas going on, but the basic message here is that smoking is bad and also Jackie Chan is going to be judging them and picking the best one.

At first I'm mostly thinking about how good a cigarette would taste right now, but then I start to look at these posters. I start to really look at them and I see there's something special here. Something I've never seen before.

You look at a few and you can tell some kids understand proportions, some might even understand perspective, but none of them get all of it. Even the kids that get it, don't get it. One might have perfect hands, but the shoes are like trapezoids. One kid drew the filter, but made the cigarette as tall as the guy smoking it. You can pick any two pictures and they'll be different, but similarly fucked.

I'm not even thinking about cigarettes anymore, I'm

mesmerized looking at these pictures. I'm looking at them so much and having such a great time I start to think I might like to do this later at home. But the drawings are here and my home is at home so I know this won't work for me. I try taking a photo, but the instant I snap one I know a facsimile won't do. I need the real thing.

I'm way past cigarettes now. Now I'm plotting on how to transition some of these masterpieces from the window back to my house. Using my brain's imagination I conjure up a scenario where I walk in and try to purchase one, but it doesn't go so well.

I imagine walking in and telling the school administrator how much I admire the work of Timothy, age 8, and Margery, age 9, and how I admire them so much I would love to pay a large cash sum to take them home. There's not really a precedent set for buying a student's art even if it is kind of being displayed so I imagine the administrator being uncomfortable and telling me "no."

But I need these drawings so I ask again and this time really emphasize how much I like the one with the weird shoes and how I would even *overpay* to close this deal right now. The woman behind the desk isn't responding positively. It's becoming clear that money isn't the issue here and my enthusiasm for the drawings is hurting me more than helping me.

Now she's *begging* me to leave and to stop talking about Timothy, age 8, and telling me there are **cameras** in this school and I'm saying, "Why are you telling me there are cameras in the school it seems like you think I'm here for a much more sinister purpose than purchasing art because I don't care if I'm on camera purchasing art. You can point a hundred cameras at me while I purchase art. That means nothing to me. But if you think I'm here to do something that I **don't want** on camera then you're highly mistaken," and then she calls the cops.

I imagine all this and decide the outcome is not desirable so I'll try something else. I start to think about how smart I am. Even though these drawings are sublime they're still made by kids and kids are so dumb. I bet if I look at them long enough and **I** get to practicing I could probably draw exactly like these kids. That's a much better plan and nobody called the cops on me when I imagined it so that's what I did and that's what I'm doing.

WOMAN: You admire children's artwork so much that you want it in your home, but you don't think you could buy it because the school would think you're trying to get close to the kids for the wrong reasons, even though you just like the artwork. So you're painting bad *on purpose* to recreate it.

ARTIST: Exactly.

ARTIST: I'm not a pedophile by the way.

WOMAN: Ok.

ARTIST: I kind of explained that part in the story, but I just want to affirm that. I'm not that.

WOMAN: I didn't think you were.

ARTIST: Good. Because that was the part in the story where things took a turn for me obviously. When the girl started thinking I was one—and now you—it's good that no one thinks I'm a pedophile.

WOMAN: I don't.

ARTIST: Not that it's good that no one thinks that because I am one. It's not like I am a pedophile and I don't want anyone to detect it. I'm not worried about being caught, you know? I'm a regular guy who's not a pedophile and I don't want people to think that I am a pedophile, because I'm not one.

WOMAN: ...

ARTIST: I actually lost my virginity when I was 21 so I'm really less of a pedophile than most people because I never even had sex with any kids when I was a kid. Although that would have been legal and fine it's still something to consider and be weighed in my favor when evaluating my status... as a pedophile.

GLAUCON: Where is the cave in this story Socrates.

WOMAN: Can I be honest.

ARTIST: Yes.

WOMAN: Before you started talking I did not think you were a pedophile. I just thought you were a bad artist. If I had to assign a percentage to how much I thought you were a pedophile it would be less than one percent. I know you may have wanted a rating of zero percent, but now that I'm thinking about it less than one percent is probably the standard rating for a normal stranger which is what you are. So you had a normal probable pedophile percentage.

ARTIST: Good. That's good news.

WOMAN: But then you started talking and... the percentage went up. I don't know what it is now. This is the most thought I've ever put into something like this. But whatever yours is, it's more than one percent.

ARTIST: Ok. Please tell what my percentage is.

WOMAN: I don't-I don't think I wanna do that.

ARTIST: Just tell me the percentage.

WOMAN: I don't want to.

ARTIST: Just tell me. If you're worried I'm going to be angry I'm not going to be.

WOMAN: Maybe, like, fifteen percent.

ARTIST: Ok, I am a bit angry. Fifteen percent? Are you serious? Were you listening to me at all? I told a story about not being a pedophile and somehow you think there's a fifteen percent chance that I am a pedophile? Were you listening to me? At all???

WOMAN: ....

ARTIST: 15 percent is basically one in six. You roll a die and think that's the same probability as me fucking a kid?

WOMAN: I don't know.

ARTIST: Oh, now you don't know?? You seemed like you knew everything a few seconds ago!! I can't believe you said fifteen percent. Fifteen percent—I'm fucked up. This is all fucked up. Were you even listening to me at all??

WOMAN: I'm leaving.

ARTIST: Hahaha no. We need to clear this up. We need to clear all of this up. Fifteen percent. Listen, I've got a way to clear all of this up. Look at this.

[*The Artist takes out his Green 512GB iPhone 13 Pro Max*]

ARTIST: We'll clear all of this up right now, gimme a sec. I've got some child porn here—

WOMAN: Oh my god.

ARTIST: —and I'm going to take a look at it. **You** be the judge if I'm getting aroused. A pedophile would feel something if they looked at child porn right? Well I'll look at it, you'll see that it does nothing for me, and that should clear all of this up.

WOMAN: I'm feeling like maybe 100% you're a pedophile.

ARTIST: Nonsense, I'm pulling it up now.

WOMAN: Pull it down.

ARTIST: I'm gonna clear this up. I'll take a quick look—a glance—and it'll be nothing. I'm a normal guy who doesn't even like this type of stuff. So it shouldn't be a problem for me take a quick peak and go about my day. Ahh ok, here we go. Got it. Pressing play. Now you'll see.

[*The Artist instantly gets a boner*]

WOMAN: Oh my god.

ARTIST: Ahh. Listen. You see the thing. I was. I was looking at this stuff—I was looking at this stuff I **don't like** and I. I accidentally thought about some **adult** sized titties. And that's why. This has occurred.

[*The Woman leaves*]

ARTIST: Ahhh, almost. I almost tricked her. Bet it all on one big hand and just barely missed. Close one. Almost. Can't win em all. Came close though. Close but no cigar. Ahh drat.

[*The Artist turns and puts his hands in his pockets. He tries to kick a rock, but misses and stumbles. He kind of parlays the stumble into an awkward step so maybe if anyone was watching they would think he just took a weird step and didn't miss kicking a rock, but no one is watching*]

PART THREE:
RETURN TO THE CAVE

GLAUCON: Wow.

SOCRATES: Yes. Now what did you learn?

GLAUCON: Hmmmm.

SOCRATES: You should have learned something.

GLAUCON: I know. I'm just. Trying to think of what I learned. Really soaking the whole thing up. Trying to parse it all out.

SOCRATES: Yes.

GLAUCON: Letting it all sink in.

SOCRATES: Start with the allegory

GLAUCON: Of course. The allegory. That's what I was abouttosay—the allegory. Ok. I need to smoke a cigarette really quick.

SOCRATES: Ok.

[*Glaucon leaves*]

[*Socrates lights a fire and uses his hands to make a shadow puppet of a girl dancing*]

SOCRATES: God I wish there were some girls in here.

2018 PRESS JUNKET - DENZEL WASHINGTON

INTERVIEWER: Mr. Washington, it's an honor. Thank you for joining us.

DENZEL WASHINGTON: Mr. Washington? You think you're in the principal's office or something?

INT: Oh my god, no. I'm sorry. My producer told me you prefer that. Is Denzel better?

WASHINGTON: Mr. Washington... [Denzel laughs] Think your producer was pulling your leg.

[Laughter off camera]

INT: Yeah, it seems like that might be the case. Sorry, about that. Ok, *Equalizer*.

WASHINGTON: *Equalizer 2.*

INT: *The Equalizer 2*, yes. Didn't think I'd be embarrassing myself quite this much before breakfast today.

WASHINGTON: Before breakfast? Can we get this guy a bagel or something?

[A PA begins to bring over a bagel]

INT: No really, I'm fine. I'm fine. We've got limited time and I've already wasted too much of it. Denzel! You are not shy about your respect for the 1985 series that these movies are based on. I've seen the show myself and these films feels like a true adaptation of the soul of the original.

WASHINGTON: Thank you, thank you.

INT: Are there any other shows or films you think *The Equalizer* series draws from?

WASHINGTON: You know, besides the original I'm not too sure. I think Antoine, Wenk, Todd Black, everyone did such a great job injecting this with the modernity it needs to be popular while also keeping the longtime fans happy.

INT: I ask because I was speaking to someone from the *Ballers* cast a few weeks ago and he mentioned that his show was fairly popular with you on set while filming *Equalizer 2*.

WASHINGTON: *Ballers*, huh? Well yes, there's one cast member I'm a bit partial to. I may have had a few episodes playing in the trailer while shooting this.

INT: I have to ask, any plans on working with John in the future?

WASHINGTON: John's his own man! Should be asking him when he's gonna work with his dad!

INT: I should have! Hopefully I'll get the chance next time.

WASHINGTON: I hope you do, I hope you do. Kids are great man. I wanted more though. Always wanted more kids.

INT: Four wasn't enough?

WASHINGTON: Four? Not even close. Not even close. What I really wanted was 19 kids. Wanted to have 19 kids all at the same time. All boys. I'll tell you what I wanted. I get something like 40 girls and I fuck em all. Get them all pregnant within a week or so. I'd do forty in case some of em come out as girls. I do that and nine months later I got around 19 sons all by different women.

INT: 19 kids seems like a lot.

WASHINGTON: It does seem like a lot, don't it? But it's only 19 at the start. The whole reason, the whole idea behind 19 kids is I wanna knock em down every year. Every year we lose one. So let's say I get my kids together and after one year we see who's saying words. Who knows the most words. We check em out and find the kid who hasn't said anything yet. The worst in the group and we dump em.

INT: Dump em?

WASHINGTON: Dump em, yeah. We lose that kid. So now

we're at 18. Another year goes by and we test them all again. This time on whatever two year olds are supposed to be good at. Eating with a spoon or walking or whatever. The early tests aren't gonna be that interesting, but you get the idea, right? Eventually we'll be testing them more physically. Who can run the fastest, jump the highest. Test them on cognitive abilities, memory recall. Maybe give them all guitars one year and we knock off who's the worst at that.

INT: When you say, "knock off." What exactly do you mean by that?

WASHINGTON: So we keep testing them and testing them. Who can bench the most. Who can learn the most languages. Who can fucking—I don't know—who can survive the longest in the wilderness. But you see after 18 years we have two kids left. Two kids that have had their skills pushed to the absolute limit. So we take these two kids. We take these two warriors and put them in a pit. We put them in a pit and only one walks out. And whoever walks out, that's my son. That's my boy.

INT: So you have your son. This theoretical perfect son. Do you worry about the toll this upbringing would have on him? All this work to raise him and I think most people would view this as another form of killing him. I think there's a huge chance he resents you for turning his life into an experiment and his siblings into his enemies. What if you look into his eyes for a child's love and all that stares back is a soldier?

WASHINGTON: What's wrong with a soldier? We used to want our sons to be soldiers. We put men in the coliseum and turned them into gods on earth. It's pressure. Pressure is what makes a man. I look around outside and all I see is wasted potential. People who lifted five pounds and never tried to lift ten. I see it in you, I see it in me, but I won't see it in my boy.

INT: It's certainly an interesting idea.

WASHINGTON: Get this. So I told you about the boys. Now imagine somewhere across the country I have 19 daughters and I'm doing the same thing with them. Now I have *two* perfect children. Son and Daughter. Outlasted all competition. Total specimens. Then I make them fuck.

INT: You make your son and daughter fuck.

WASHINGTON: They have different mothers so they're only half-siblings. They can fuck. Imagine that kid though. Holy shit. Wow. Doesn't matter though. Wife didn't let me do any of this. She wasn't into it. That's why we just had the four.

INT: You've got a wonderful family.

WASHINGTON: All the women. They'd all be white jawns too. White ones.

INT: Ok. Anything else you'd like to add that you feel like we didn't cover?

WASHINGTON: I can. I can tell if her pussys wet just by touching it.

Cool Nicknames to Have in the Army

Bullet Engineer
Murder God
3 Gun Chun
Angel of Pain
The Warrior of Light
God's Warrior
God's Deadliest Warrior
God's Champion
Metal Sender
Metal Falcon
Metal Falcon DX
Dirt Monster
Slug Master
Long Gun Chun
The Decider
Orphan Maker
Orphan Creator
Orphan Manufacturer
The Orphan Factory
Deadeye
Wild Dog
Stroker
The Orphanator
Murderangelo
Demontello
The Creature
Whole Hog Henry
Concrete Fingers
Hole Maker
Mom Sniper
Seven Six Screw
Razor
The Razor
The Holy Reckoning
Dawnbringer

God's Messenger
Jungle Demon
Big Gun Chun
Cutthroat
Soul Breaker
Mega Naruto
The Butcher
Westside Wayne
Slaughter Spouse Five
Little Man
Little Big Man
Psycho Butcher
Wife Killer
Phantom X
Heaven's Vengeance
Goat Sucker
Heart Stopper
Life Ender
Boner
Firestorm
Stone Heart
Bone Powder
Kill Master
Twist
Big Lemon
Child Hunter
Carpet Shark
Hammer
Captain Kill
The Executioner
Goblin Judge
Man Halver
The User
The Abuser
Machine Gun Chun

MOVIE / TV IDEAS

Movie Ideas (Organic vs AI)

Here are 23 original movie ideas and three generated by AI.

I am not worried.

Original Ideas

1. A veteran prostitute meets a client who's so good at sex she starts paying to fuck him (R-rated).

2. A balding/failing salesman becomes addicted to getting stuck in elevators with strangers.

3. A new HOA rule that requires homeowners to fit their property with a scarecrow is turned upside down when one rule-breaker pays a vagrant to drink on his lawn 24/7.

4. A young man moves his hands back and forth.

5. An injured D1 basketball player starts a business selling his down syndrome brother's clean urine to other collegiate athletes.

6. A Wall Street banker makes a bet with a colleague that he can turn a homeless man inside out.

7. The most popular girl in school befriends an elderly neighbor during court-mandated community service and he doesn't do anything weird to her.

8. A recent suburban divorcé can only regain custody of his son if he wins a breakdance competition in the hood.

9. It's a tie game going into the 4th quarter of the last Super Bowl when the rapture starts happening.

10. A girl with big tits and a huge ass.

11. A law school dropout uncovers a legal loophole that allows him to buy three energy drinks for the price of one.

12. A disillusioned young man learns to be himself until he meets a cooler man and learns it might be better to try and be more like him.

13. A disgraced former baseball star is given a chance to hit the most important home run of his career when an asteroid the size of a baseball punctures Earth's atmosphere.

14. 44 dead, 1,100 wounded.

15. An immigrant woman trafficked into sex slavery discovers the healing powers of improv comedy.

16. A toddler's life is turned upside down when her new nanny starts shaking her.

17. An American ex-pat in Japan competes in a country-wide karaoke contest to pay his wife's drunk driving debts.

18. A special olympics coach tries not to laugh.

19. The secrets of King Tut are revealed to all who will listen.

20. Two high school English teachers discover they've each been molesting the same student (boy student for comedy, girl student for drama).

21. The king's fiercest torturer meets his match: Jesus Christ.

22. A frustrated father begins administering Trenbolone to his theater obsessed middle school son in an attempt to make him more regular.

23. A recent retiree joins a bodybuilding gym to prepare for the biggest challenge of his life: killing his wife.

AI Ideas

Echoes of Tomorrow - Sci-Fi YA Thriller

"In a world where virtual reality has become a dominant force, a group of teenagers discovers a glitch in the system that allows them to travel back in time through their VR headsets. They find themselves in a high-stakes race against time to prevent a catastrophic event that could alter the future. As they navigate different historical eras, they must not only overcome numerous challenges but also confront personal struggles and learn valuable lessons about friendship, bravery, and the consequences of their actions."

–Sounds like garbage shit

Bro-Cation - Comedy

"Follow the hilarious misadventures of two best friends, Jake and Ryan, who embark on an epic road trip to escape their mundane lives and reconnect before one of them ties the knot. However, their well-intentioned trip takes an unexpected turn when they accidentally stumble upon a hidden treasure map. Determined to strike it rich, they find themselves in a series of outrageous situations, encountering quirky characters, rival treasure hunters, and unforeseen obstacles along the way. As their friendship is tested, they must rely on their wit, camaraderie, and absurd improvisation skills to survive the journey and make it back home in time for the wedding."

–Sounds like garbage shit

Love in Full Bloom - Romance

"Welcome to the enchanting story of Emma, a vibrant and independent woman in her late twenties, who unexpectedly inherits a beautiful flower shop in a quaint town. Determined to make a fresh start, Emma pours her heart into revitalizing the struggling business, and in the process, she crosses paths with Ethan, a talented but jaded landscape artist. As they collaborate on a grand floral exhibition, their initial clashes evolve into a blossoming friendship and a slow-burning romance. However, their personal fears, past heartbreaks, and conflicting aspirations threaten to derail their burgeoning relationship. Against a backdrop of vibrant blooms and heartfelt conversations, they must learn to trust each other and embrace the power of love to heal and grow."

-Has potential with the right director I might lie and say I made this up

TV Ideas

Is She a Gusher for Usher?
ALT Title: *Will Your Girlfriend Fuck Usher?*

Elevator Pitch: Hidden camera reality show tests relationships by seeing if supposedly loyal girlfriends will fuck American singer/songwriter Usher.

Girls in serious relationships are secretly filmed in manipulated setups where they are able to meet Usher. Through three acts they are tested while their significant other watches live in a control room with the host (host should not be white).

If the girl stays loyal the couple wins an all expenses paid lover's vacation. If she folds and fucks Usher the boyfriend is given the chance to confront her on live television.

Different setups where girls meet Usher could be after a concert, at a club, at the gas station, or at Buffalo Wild Wings (potential crossover promotion).

There will be three acts where the girl is given propositions by Usher that start as platonic, but escalate to potential infidelity. In the first stage Usher would ask her to come somewhere public with him. Second stage is asking her to go somewhere private. Third and final stage is explicit sexual activity.

Possible Hooks/Viral Moments

-Girl texts boyfriend "OMG, I just met USHER," not knowing that the boyfriend is watching all of this live. Then as Usher invites her back to his hotel she stops texting her boyfriend while he watches the disaster unfold.

-Usher asks girl if she has a boyfriend. She replies, "no," all while her boyfriend watches in horror.

-Usher isolates the girlfriend in a hotel suite and leans in to kiss her. She kisses him back hard and tells him how bad she wants to feel him inside her. Usher says he needs to pee and get a condom so he leaves the room. Boyfriend then enters and is given the chance to confront her.

-If the boyfriend became violent we would most likely stop it.

Fat Guy Combine
Alt Title: *LOLympics*

Elevator Pitch: The NFL combine is exciting, but too familiar/predictable. Let's do a combine where everyone is fat to find the most in-shape out-of-shape guy.

We bring in like 12 fatsos and see how high they can jump, how fast they run a 40, make em do the 3-cone drill. Lol.

Possible Hooks/Viral Moments

-They're gonna get hurt they're big fellas.

-Reduce the time between events. They should be doing the whole combine in like 30 minutes.

-Maybe we don't let them have any water. Say there was a mishap with the water and it's coming later. Let them have coffee in the meantime. They can have as many cups of coffee as they want.

-Winner gets to choose between $25,000 or a big bowl of ice cream. I'm kidding we won't do that.

Celebrity Sex Match
ALT Title: *Fucking with the Stars*

Elevator Pitch: Contestants are given the opportunity/challenge to fuck celebrities and see if they can make them cum within a certain time limit.

Not much else to say. We put a regular person and a celebrity in a room and they fuck while the clock counts down. If the celebrity cums within the time limit the contestant wins.

Possible trouble could occur if the celebrity was trying as hard as they could not to cum? Like they were really not into it on purpose? Not sure how we would fix that. They just have to be a good sport I suppose.

I honestly believe this will be a real show within twenty years.

Possible Hooks/Viral Moments

-This is pornography.

Front Line Cook
ALT Title: *War Chef: Battlegrounds*

Elevator Pitch: You've seen chefs cook from the comfort of the kitchen, but how will they fare in the blood-soaked reality of the battlefield.

Ten chefs are dropped into an active war zone with nothing but their favorite vegetables and spices. While under assault from snipers, white phosphorous, and hunter-killer drones, these culinary artists must plate a dish that not only wows the judges, but also sustains a group of freedom-fighters during their doomed to fail ground campaign.

Possible Hooks / Viral Moments

-Contestants attempt to communicate crucial kitchen instructions to their teammates under the hail of gunfire.

-A chef tries to make flan while an MQ-9 Reaper drops hellfire missiles around him.

-Some of them get voted off and others just die.

Trade Trade
ALT Title: *Honey, I Had A Crazy Day at the Office*

Elevator Pitch: Who has the hardest job in America? Let's find out each week when two hard-working Americans swap occupations for 48 hours. Every episode one of the jobs is "Guy Who Gets Fucked in the Ass" though.

Writes itself. Bring in some tough oil rig worker and let him preach about how hard his job is. Then tell him his new job is Guy Who Gets Fucked in the Ass. Bet he doesn't think his job is so tough then.

Hilarious fish out of water TV. Not sure about discrimination laws, but for obvious reasons we might not be able to cast gay men or certain straight men.

Possible Hooks/Viral Moments

-It will mostly be that one moment where the guy is informed of the job he is switching to. The parts after where he is actually doing the job will be less interesting.

Doggy Day Scare
ALT Title: *Don't need one this is perfect*

Elevator Pitch: Gag show where regular people picking up their dogs from day care are told that their dog got squashed and died.

No build up at all. Just 23 straight minutes of people walking up to the counter and getting told their dog is dead.

"Hi, I'm here to pick up my dog, Gandalf :)"

"Ohhhh, so sorry, your Gandalf got squashed today :("

Could potentially fit ~30 or so pranks into each episode.

Possible Hooks / Viral Moments

-Pet owners love their pets so they will most likely freak out when they are told their pet died which could make for a hilarious viral moment.

-When owner starts to freak have receptionist point to a sign that says "We are not responsible for anything that happens here."

-Tell owner that their dog is dead and they lose it. Then the receptionist re-reads the computer and goes, "Oh no, I'm so sorry. That was someone else's dog. My mistake. What's your dogs name again?"
They'll be relieved because they believe their dog is still alive and not dead. Then have receptionist go, "Oh wait. I'm sorry, but your dog got squashed and died too." The twists and turns here will keep everyone guessing.

-Bring dog into hallway for reunion with owner and have giant Indiana Jones-style boulder roll through building and crush the beast. Have employee say something like, "Oh no."

-Most of the time it's a prank and we are not squashing the dogs for real.

2013 PRESS JUNKET - BRAD PITT

INTERVIEWER: Brad. Bradley. How are you?

BRAD PITT: Just Brad. Or William I guess.

INT: Brad. Great to see you again. Let me just say it, I loved *World War Z*.

PITT: Yeah. You see this?

INT: See what?

PITT: There's like. Hella gay people outside.

INT: Oh. Ok.

PITT: Like a lot of them.

INT: That's LA for you.

PITT: You seen *Seinfeld*? It's like when all the Puerto Ricans are outside in the *Seinfeld* episode.

INT: Oh, like a parade? Oh! June! Yeah, of course it's Pride. That's what's going on.

PITT: Oh yeah? That makes sense.

INT: Have you been?

PITT: To Pride? No. Nah, I don't think so.

INT: It's a good time. My first year in LA I went with a roommate. Lots of fun. Great time.

PITT: Yeah. I don't know.

INT: You should go. I think you'd really enjoy yourself.

PITT: Probably... it feels a bit like going to a concert where you don't know any of the songs though. You might have an alright time, but nothing compared to the guys that know all the words. These guys have been listening to the songs their whole life and I've never heard one. That's who the concert is for. Not me.

INT: You don't have to be gay to go to Pride. It's all inclusive. It's for everyone, show support, be an ally.

PITT: For sure. I know. Definitely gotta be an ally. I just think the real fans would rather be surrounded by other real fans, right? You ever been to a concert and get up to the front row and there are people on their phones? Not dancing? Like what the fuck are you doing at the concert if you're not about to wild out with me? You're in the wrong place. If I'm in a spot I wanna really be in there. Not like a tortoise.

INT: A tortoise?

PITT: Tourist. I meant to say tourist. Did you really like *World War Z*?

INT: I liked the book.

PITT: I hear that so much it makes me not want to read it.

8TH STREET

EXT. STREET - NIGHT

> GIRL 1
> We shouldn't be out this late.

> GIRL 2
> It's not that late.

> GIRL 1
> After dark is late. Don't you watch
> the news? They still haven't caught
> the 8th Street Rapist. He struck
> again last night.

> GIRL 2
> No. And this is 9th street.

> GIRL 1
> He doesn't only rape on 8th street.

> GIRL 2
> I would hope he'd be caught by now
> if he did.

GIRL 1

It's just a name. They have to call
him something. He caught his first
victim walking home on 8th street
and boom, "8th Street Rapist." He
has the whole city paralyzed with
fear.

GIRL 2

I don't feel paralyzed.

GIRL 1

If you watched the news more you
would be. I haven't been out for
weeks.

GIRL 2

So, why are we out tonight?

GIRL 1

I couldn't let you go alone. You
haven't taken the self-defense
course. You won't know what to do
if you run into that psycho.

GIRL 2

Please advise me.

GIRL 1

The instructor said the best
strategy against a criminal is to
remain calm, do not resist, and
give them what they ask for.

GIRL 2

This seems like a poor strategy
against the 8th Street Rapist.

GIRL 1

That's what I thought too. So I
took her plan and I'm modifying it.
I'll still remain calm, not resist,
but I'm changing the last step from
"give them what they ask for" to
"act disabled."

GIRL 2
(choking on laughter)
You're going to act retarded to
stop a rapist.

GIRL 1

STOP. IT WOULD WORK! And don't say
the r-word it's not nice.

GIRL 2

You think if you start drooling on
yourself his heart will grow three
sizes and he'll spare you.

GIRL 1

I'm not gonna drool on myself. What
do you think disabled people are
like? You're so insensitive.

GIRL 2

I'm insensitive? Show me. Please.
How do you plan on "acting
ret—**disabled.**"

GIRL 1
It's like. I'll talk weird—

GIRL 2

Talk weird?

                    GIRL 1
LIKE RAIN MAN OK. I'll start getting
fidgety and twitch and talk like
really specific about something,
like how many blue cars are on the
street, but also like, I don't know
what's going on.

                    GIRL 2
Rain Man was autistic, he wasn't
retarded. Your big plan is to act
autistic?

                    GIRL 1
At least I have a plan. I have a
three step plan. Honestly, you're
lucky I came with you tonight.

                    GIRL 2
You're right. I'm very lucky.
Alright, this is it.

Girl 2 knocks on a window.

                    GIRL 1
Did you text him?

                    GIRL 2
Yeah, like five minutes ago.

Girl 2 knocks on the window again.

                    GIRL 2
It's us.

                    GIRL 1
Hii.

The window slides open an inch.

                    JUMBO
          What.

                    GIRL 2
          I texted you.

                    JUMBO
          You shouldn't be out this late. The
          whole city's paralyzed with fear.

The window slams shut. Door unlocks.

INT. JUMBO'S HOUSE - CONTINUOUS

Jumbo smokes a cig and peers through
the blinds.

                    JUMBO
          They're saying he's Estonian.

                    GIRL 2
          Who?

                    JUMBO
          You know who.

Jumbo shuts the blinds.

                    GIRL 2
          Oh.

                    GIRL 1
          I didn't see that on the news.

                    JUMBO
Yeah, they wouldn't put it out there.
Don't want to cause a mass panic.
But I have it from a credible source
the 8th Street Rapist is Estonian.
If you see someone from Estonia...
offense is better than defense.

                    GIRL 1
Where's Estonia?

                    JUMBO
Fuck do I look like I gotta fucking
map or something? I'm giving **you**
the information. What **you** do with
it is up to you.

                    GIRL 1
What does someone from Estonia look
like?

                    JUMBO
Imagine someone from Latvia but
different.

                    GIRL 2
Should we be profiling all Estonians
because of one guy? This going to
wreak havoc on Little Estonia.

                    JUMBO
In times like these we must employ
all possible defense tactics
including racism.

                    GIRL 1
Thank you, Jumbo.

                    JUMBO
No problem. What do you need.

                    GIRL 2
G and a Max pass please.

                    JUMBO
$80 and $15 for the login. Should
be good for another six months.
Fucking waste of money, one of you
should learn how to torrent.

                    GIRL 2
No :)

Jumbo takes her money and rummages in a
drawer for a baggie.

                 TELEVISION
                    (v.o.)
—the Police Commissioner has issued
a new statement regarding the ever-
growing victim pool and draught
of leads, "We are really trying
to get this guy. I swear we are."
Comforting words from our fearless—

                    JUMBO
Yeah.

Jumbo hands Girl 2 a baggie and a folded
notecard.

                    GIRL 1
We should go. We shouldn't be out
this late.

EXT. STREETS - NIGHT

                    GIRL 1
          Should we run?

                    GIRL 2
          No.

                    GIRL 1
          We'd get home faster if we ran.

                    GIRL 2
          No.

A cloaked man appears from the shadows.

               THE PROTECTOR OF THE REALM
          HALT! IDENTIFY YOURSELVES!

                    GIRL 1
          AHHHHHHHHHHH!!!

                    GIRL 2
          No.

               THE PROTECTOR OF THE REALM
          YOU SHOULDN'T BE OUT THIS LATE. THE
          CITY IS PARALYZED WITH FEAR.

                    GIRL 2
          What are you doing.

               THE PROTECTOR OF THE REALM
          PROTECTING THE REALM.

                    GIRL 1
          Are you Estonian?

                    THE PROTECTOR OF THE REALM
NO.

                         GIRL 1
I think we're safe.

                         GIRL 2
Thank god.

          THE PROTECTOR OF THE REALM
WHAT IS YOUR BUSINESS HERE AT THE
CROSS? WHAT IS YOUR DESTINATION?

                         GIRL 2
Our   business   is   kind   of...our
business?

                         GIRL 1
Don't think it's a good time to
tell strangers where we're headed.
I'm sure you can understand that
given your line of work.

          THE PROTECTOR OF THE REALM
VERY GOOD.
     (beat)
THAT WAS A TEST.

                         GIRL 2
Ok.

          THE PROTECTOR OF THE REALM
BUT NOW YOU MUST ANSWER THIS RIDDLE
TO PASS.

A more normal guy jogs up the street.

                    VIGILANTE LEADER
Is everything ok here? I heard
screams.

                         GIRL 1
I suck at riddles.

                         GIRL 2
We're in the middle of something.

                    VIGILANTE LEADER
Sorry, don't mean to disturb you
two. You can go, you don't need
to answer a riddle. We just talked
about this actually you shouldn't
be asking riddl—

          THE PROTECTOR OF THE REALM
I AM ALWAYS HUNGRY. I'LL DIE IF NOT
FED. BUT IF I AM TOUCHED. YOU'LL
SURELY TURN RED. WHAT AM I?

                         GIRL 1
A fat guy?

                         GIRL 2
Fire.

          THE PROTECTOR OF THE REALM
PROCEED.

                    VIGILANTE LEADER
Yeah, sorry again. We're doing what
we can to help, but it's not easy.
You work with what you get.

                         GIRL 2
I feel much safer now, thank you.

                    GIRL 1
So, what are you doing? You're like
in a gang or something?

                VIGILANTE LEADER
We're a group of like minded citizens
who see our leaders failing us.
Police say they're doing all they
can, but it feels more like the
bare minimum. People are scared
to leave their homes at night and
this psycho is no closer to being
caught. The whole city's paralyzed
with fear.

                    GIRL 2
Yeah, I've been hearing that.

                    GIRL 1
Well thank you for your hard work.

            THE PROTECTOR OF THE REALM
NO PROBLEM.

                VIGILANTE LEADER
Will you join us? The city is
stronger together. We could use the
help.

                    GIRL 2
We're committed to another citizen
sentry group.

                    VIGILANTE LEADER
Keep an eye open and stay safe
then. If you do happen to get into
trouble the police won't help. It's
best to alert our group with the
secret signal.

                    GIRL 1
What's that?

                    VIGILANTE LEADER
Screaming.

                    GIRL 2
Got it.

EXT. ALLEY - NIGHT

                    GIRL 1
We've gotta be close now.

                    GIRL 2
We'd be closer if we walked up 8th
instead of this alley.

                    GIRL 1
You're insane if you think I'm
walking on 8th street. That's **the**
street. That he's rapi—

                    GIRL 2
Eughhh, at least 8th Street is an
actual street. There are lights.
There are buildings with doors.
Human population. This is a fucking
alley. Say whatever about 8th street,
but there are far less human shits
there.

                    GRAVELY VOICE
          (o.s.)
I'm not shitting back here.

                       GIRL 1
AHHHHHHHHHHHHH!!

Girl 2 shines her phone light behind a
dumpster to illuminate a squatting smoking
woman.

                       GIRL 1
Fuck, you scared me! What are you
doing back here?

                       GIRL 2
Shitting.

                    PROSTITUTE
I'm not shitting.

                       GIRL 1
You shouldn't be out this late.
Don't you know what's going on?

                    PROSTITUTE
Yeah, I know a thing or two about
what's going on.

                       GIRL 1
Are you...

                       GIRL 2
Working?

                    PROSTITUTE
Not as much as I'd like to be. Current
events not great for business.

GIRL 1
So, you're not scared?

PROSTITUTE
Scared? Of course I'm scared. But you know what's scarier? Not eating. Not paying rent. Going back to the shelter.

GIRL 1
You know what **I** think is scary? Getting fucking rap—

GIRL 2
Have you seen anything out here? Have you known any of the girls?

PROSTITUTE
It's been going on for months now. Everybody working knows somebody.
     (beat)
Anastasia. She was early on. I lived with her for a few months in the beginning of the year.

GIRL 1
Jesus. I'm sorry.

PROSTITUTE
We were both staying at this cam house. Loads of livestream setups in the basement. She'd work those most nights, but she'd go out too. Do dates.

GIRL 2
What happened?

                    PROSTITUTE
Got in a car she shouldn't have.
Maybe she didn't even get in. Who
knows. He could have forced her.
She turned up 25 miles outside the
city handcuffed in a ditch. Alive,
but in a ditch. I only heard about
it from another girl at the house,
haven't seen her since.

                      GIRL 1
Fuuck. I'm sorry, but it's insane
that you're still out here. How are
you still working with this freak
on the loose?

                    PROSTIUTE
You   can't   spend   every   moment
thinking about the worst that can
happen. You think cops can do their
job if they're scared to take a
bullet? That's no way to live. It's
always been like this. A little
louder now, more media coverage,
but it's always been like this.

                      GIRL 2
I think most cops are scared to
take a bullet, but yeah, I get what
you mean.

The prostitute takes a long drag of her
cigarette.

                    PROSTITUTE
I saw him a few days ago.

GIRL 1

Him?

PROSTITUTE

I think it was him at least. This guy
was sitting in this old ass Altima.
Like 6:00 AM. Far from 8th street
too, I don't know why they fucking
call him that when he's grabbing
girls all over. Anyway, he's parked
on the far side of the street but
he's sitting in the passenger seat.
Window is cracked an inch and he's
just staring through the glass at
me and a few other girls wrapping
up the night.

GIRL 2

So what happened?

PROSTITUTE

Nothing. He kept staring. Then he
slid over to the driver seat and
took off.

GIRL 1

How did you know it was him?

PROSTITUTE

Just could feel it. There's a
nervousness about certain johns
and a familiarity with other ones.
I couldn't feel either with him.
		(she smokes more)
I don't know maybe he was just a
weirdo.

                    GIRL 2
We'll watch out for Altimas then.
Thanks for sharing.

                    GIRL 1
You be safe out there.

                   PROSTIUTE
I know what I'm doing.
          (she shows a switchblade)
You two are the ones that need to
be careful.

              HIGH PITCHED VOICE
              (o.s.)
AHHHHHHHHHHHHHHHH!!! AHHhH!

                    GIRL 1
That's the signal! Someone's in
trouble.

                  MALE VOICE
              (o.s.)
HEY!! HEY! THAT'S FUCKING HIM!!
STOP HIM!

BOOM! A gun shot rings out.

The Prostitute takes off running.

                 MALE VOICE 2
              (o.s.)
STOP HIM!!

A bunch of vigilantes run through the alley.

               VIGILANTE LEADER
Which way did he go??

                    GIRL 1
We didn't see anything.

                    GIRL 2
Was someone shooting?

                 VIGILANTE 1
He was seen running through this
alley, are you sure you didn't see
anything?

                 VIGILANTE 2
I heard someone on the fire escape,
he could be on the roof by now.

              VIGILANTE LEADER
Send two guys up the escape.
Everyone in pairs. WE ARE CATCHING
HIM TONIGHT.

                    GIRL 2
We'll leave you to it.

              VIGILANTE LEADER
No. I apologize, but in good
conscious I can't allow you two
to leave without an escort. A new
victim was just discovered on 8th
street 20 minutes ago. We're hot on
his trail now.

                    GIRL 1
So, you're keeping us against our
will. In the alley.

              VIGILANTE LEADER
Yes.

                    VIGILANTE 1
For your safety.

                     GIRL 2
Thank you, but I think we'd feel
safer almost anywhere else.

                    VIGILANTE 2
You're welcome.

More vigilantes rush in from the opposite
end.

                    VIGILANTE 3
Did you get him?

                 VIGILANTE LEADER
He's not here. You didn't see him
on your end?

                HIGH PITCHED VOICE
                    (o.s.)
HEEELPP!!! AHHHHH!

               HIGH PITCHED VOICE 2
                    (o.s.)
HELP!!!!

BANG! Another gun shot rings out in the
distance.

The vigilantes all rush in different directions
to follow the screams. Girl 2 grabs Girl 1
and tries to slip away in the chaos. The
girls are knocked down in the stampede.

They try to rise up, but some of the vigilantes are fighting with each other now. Total pandemonium. A gun raises out of the crowd.

BANG! More shots go off near and far. The lone alley light is blown apart. Glass rains down on the mob as darkness takes over.

EXT. ANOTHER STREET - CONTINUOUS

> GIRL 2
> Hey! Hey!! Where. The fuck. Are you??

Girl 2 takes out her phone and tries to call Girl 1.

> GIRL 2
> Pick up. Pick up.

It keeps ringing. Girl 2 stumbles down the street. She's a bit roughed up from the mob.

> GIRL 2
> Pick up pick up pick up.

> VOICE IN DARKNESS
> (o.s.)
> Try a voice mail.

> GIRL 2
> FUCK!

> VOICE IN DARKNESS
> (o.s.)
> Sorry. Didn't mean to scare you.

A homeless style dude in an army jacket is sitting on the curb.

                    ARMY MAN
You shouldn't be out this late. The
whole city's—

                    GIRL 2
Paralyzed with fear yeah I've heard
that too. Have you seen another
girl out here? My height, my size,
kind of looks like me.

                    ARMY MAN
Seen a lot of girls out here.
        (beat)
Some of them even see me too.

                    GIRL 2
Eughhh, really? I've had a fucking
night, man. I was kind of looking
for someone more normal to help me
with this.

                    ARMY MAN
Am I not normal?

                    GIRL 2
First read? No, not really.

                    ARMY MAN
That's ok. I don't think I'm normal
either. Thanks for telling me.

                    GIRL 2
No problem. Mind if I sit for a
second?

                    ARMY MAN
Please.

Girl 2 joins him on the curb and starts
texting.

                    ARMY MAN
It's not good for you to look at
that thing all day.

                    GIRL 2
How do you know I look at it all
day?

                    ARMY MAN
You all do.

                    GIRL 2
Well, you're right about that
unfortunately. I'm probably going
to look at this thing every day
until I die.

                    ARMY MAN
You're young. I should hope you have
a lot of time before that happens.

                    GIRL 2
Me too man. So, you haven't seen
anyone else around here?

                    ARMY MAN
Like you? Some. A girl in a skirt.
On the back block. Very short skirt.
I've seen her around before, not
like you.

                    GIRL 2
Skirt? I might've met her earlier.
Yeah, she's...outside a bit more
than I am. I'm looking for someone
else, her name is—

Girl 1 runs up.

                    GIRL 1
THERE YOU ARE.

                    GIRL 2
Not answering your phone?

                    GIRL 1
I lost it in the mess. Using it for
a flashlight and someone knocked it
out of my hand. I was right behind
you and then I wasn't.

                   ARMY MAN
I think I found your friend.

                    GIRL 2
Yeah, thanks for all your help
buddy.

Girl 2 stands up.

                    GIRL 1
Who's this?

                    GIRL 2
Another protector of the realm.

                    GIRL 1
Are you Estonian?

ARMY MAN
No. No sir.

GIRL 1
Great. Ok then. Can we get the fuck
out of here?

GIRL 2
Yeah, I'll stay behind you this time.
Nice to meet you, sir. You're more
normal than I originally thought.

ARMY MAN
Thank you, but I don't think I am.

HIGH PITCHED VOICE
(o.s.)
AHHHHHHHH!

GIRL 1
Oh my god, that sounds close.

HIGH PITCHED VOICE
(o.s.)
HELLLLLLLPPPP!

Girl 2 pushes Girl 1 and they run after the
voice.

ARMY MAN
Heard that before.

EXT. 8th STREET - CONTINUOUS

The girls rush out of an intersection.

They're on 8th street now.

                         GIRL 2
    Oh.

The prostitute is lying in the middle of the
street. There's blood stains on her ripped
shirt.

She looks dead.

                         GIRL 1
    We shouldn't be out this late.

The girls run over to the body. Girl 2 gets
low to her.

                         GIRL 2
    Get your phone out.

                         GIRL 1
    I don't have a fucking phone who's
    she gonna call? She's fucking dead!

                       PROSTITUTE
    Bleh, huehehu.

Girl 2 gives Girl 1 her phone. She takes off
her jacket and uses it to apply pressure to
the wound.

                         GIRL 2
    She's not dead. Call an ambulance.

                         GIRL 1
    It's busy I'm not getting anyone.

                         GIRL 2
    Go find the mob. Get someone over
    here. Do the signal!

                    GIRL 1
AHHHHHH! AAAHHHH!!!! AAAAHHHHHHHH!!
IS IT WORKING?!

                    GIRL 2
Just fucking go! Run! Find someone.

                    GIRL 1
Yeah. Ok. Are you good here? Alone??

                    GIRL 2
It's fine, those guys are around
here somewhere, but stay on the
line too in case they pick up. Tell
them we're on 8th street.

                    GIRL 1
Ok for sure. I'll be back in a
minute. I'll keep screaming.

Girl 1 takes off down the street into the
darkness.

                    GIRL 2
Stay with me. You're ok, you're
gonna be ok.

                    PROSTITUTE
Euhghhhh.

The Prostitute coughs up blood and gurgles
on it. Not looking good.

                    GIRL 2
HEY!! ANYBODY OUT THERE!?! WE NEED
SOME FUCKING HELP!!!

The Prostitute becomes less responsive. Her body fidgets a bit more. A man runs up the street.

                    MAN
     Hey-oh my god. I heard the screams.
     What can I do?

                    GIRL 2
     Do you have a car? We need to get
     her to a hospital.

                    MAN
     Oh shit. No, I just heard the
     screams and came out. Is she ok?

                    GIRL 2
     Hey, hey. How we doing?

Girl 2 slides her hand up to the Prostitute's neck to feel a pulse. She's gone.

Girl 2 moves her jacket from the wound to the back of the Prostitute's head, giving her a pillow.

                    MAN
     Oh, man. Shit. I'm so sorry.

Girl 2 gets up and sits on the curb.

                    MAN
     Did you know her?

                    GIRL 2
     Yeah. No. A bit.

                    MAN
Where are the fucking police?

                   GIRL 2
Paralyzed with fear.

                    MAN
All that screaming. You'd think
someone would've shown up by now.
I'm sorry.

                   GIRL 2
You didn't do anything.

                    MAN
It's just. I. I didn't want that to
happen.

He sits down next to Girl 2.

                    MAN
She pulled the knife first.

                   GIRL 2
What?

                    MAN
It was her knife! I didn't want to
hurt her like that, but once the
knife is out. I-I don't have a lot
of options.

Girl 2 stands up in shock.

                    MAN
That was smart to apply pressure
like that. It wasn't gonna help
though. I only got her with the

                      81

knife once. Most of it she got bad on the head. Smashed her a bit on the ground. See?

He points to the curb where Girl 2 was sitting. It's wet with blood.

                    GIRL 2
You're. You're the fucking—

                    MAN
Yeah. Can you sit back down?
          (he shows the knife)
I don't want to chase someone again.

Girl 2 slowly sits back down on the curb, further away from the man then she was originally.

                    MAN
Thanks. That means a lot.

                    GIRL 2
Police are coming. The mob is coming. My friend's on the phone with the police right now.

                    MAN
I hope they are. It's kind of stupid I got away with this for so long.

                    GIRL 2
You want to get caught?

                    MAN
It's a lot of work not getting caught. Like working two jobs. Maybe three. I could use a vacation. Some

time off.
                (beat)
I say that now, but it could be
different if I see lights. Cops come
I might change my mind, run off, do
something crazy. Hard to say until
it happens.

Girl 2 digs in her pockets, searching for
something to use as a weapon.

                    MAN
You can relax if you want. As much
as you can I mean. I'm not gonna do
anything to you.

                    GIRL 2
Comforting. You tell her the same
thing?

                    MAN
I didn't say anything to her. Didn't
do anything to her either. Until
I...you know. **She** recognized **me**.
Walked right up. Asked me where I'd
been tonight and she could tell I'd
been up to no good. Then she pulled
the knife and...

                    GIRL 2
So it was self-defense. You think
you'll get off for that?

                    MAN
Didn't really think about it, but
I guess, yeah. She initiated the
violence. She started it. I tried
to stop her. I was fighting for my

own life! I think a jury would see it my way. The other stuff not so much, but maybe this one.

                    GIRL 2
You're gonna rot in jail.

                    MAN
Yeah. No. I don't think I'm going to jail. It's been almost six months and I'm still here. This is where I took the first girl actually. Six months since I took her, in the exact same place, and...
          (he shows his wrists)
...still no cuffs.

                    GIRL 2
Everybody gets caught.

                    MAN
A lot of people do. Not everybody.

                    GIRL 2
Why.

                    MAN
Why?

                    GIRL 2
Why do you do this? Hurt women.

                    MAN
It's easier than men. Women are usually weaker and easier to hurt. Some men are as weak as women and I'll hurt them too, but yeah, mostly women I guess.

                    GIRL 2
Practical.

                    MAN
I've done a lot of men. Maybe a third
or so. From what I've seen they
don't even come forward. Doesn't
get reported. They just keep it to
themselves.

                    GIRL 2
Congratulations   to   the   least
problematic rapist.

                    MAN
Thanks. Euugggghhhhhhhh.

The man moves his shirt up a bit and reveals
a stab wound.

                    MAN
She got me pretty good before I got
her.

                    GIRL 2
You deserve worse.

                    MAN
Can you blame me? You put a lamb in
the sea do you blame the shark for
what happens?

                    GIRL 2
Yes, I fucking blame the shark,
fuck the shark.

                    MAN
Ok. I hope you're not on the jury.

                    GIRL 2
You're not seeing a jury. There's
a dozen vigilantes with guns that
somehow might be dumber than you
and I promise they're not taking
you alive.

He pokes his finger around his wound.

                    MAN
Alive might not be an option anymore.

                    GIRL 2
Are you even Estonian?

                    MAN
What's Estonian?

                    GIRL 2
It doesn't—it doesn't matter. Just
hurry up and die please. Why am I
saying please? Fucking die, dude!

She stands up and puts some space between
them.

                    MAN
Hey, take it easy. Fuuuucck.

He fumbles with the knife and drops it.
Whatever strength he showed earlier is
entirely gone. He coughs up blood.

                    MAN
Take me to a hospital.

Girl 2 picks up the knife.

                    GIRL 2
HEY!!! HE'S FUCKING HERE!! THE 8th
STREET RAPIST IS DYING IN THE STREET
HERE! I GOT HIM!!!

                    MAN
You're freaking out. Please calm
down and take me to a hospital.

                    GIRL 2
AHGHGHRHGHRHGH!!!!

Girl 2 waves her arms and screams down both
sides of the street. Empty. Nobody's coming.

                    GIRL 2
FUCK!!!

                    MAN
If you take me to a hospital... I'll
tell you where the buried treasure
is.

Girl 2 turns and soccer kicks the man in
the head. She screams one last time and sits
back down on the curb.

                    MAN
Eughghhhdz. Sh'okay. I'll admit,
d'ere is no treasure. Saw through
that quick. You got me there.

Girl 2 digs her hands in her pockets. She
fumbles a bit with her right hand, something's
in there. She takes it back out and sees...
the bag of coke.

She rolls the bag back and forth between her fingers. Then throws it across the street.

                    GIRL 2
     I shouldn't be out this late.

                    MAN
     You had that bag on you? Shit,
     bitch. Can I hit that? If you're
     not using it.

He starts crawling on his stomach towards the baggie.

                    MAN
     Dammmn, is this full?
          (he starts dabbing his pinky
          in and gumming it)
       You didn't touch this?

                    GIRL 2
     My birthday's tomorrow. Kind of
     lost the appetite.

                    MAN
     You   want   to   know   something.
     Something crazy. If I had just. Not
     done any of that stuff. None of this
     would have happened.

He tries to fit his nostril directly over the bag and flick the bottom to shoot the coke upwards.

                    GIRL 2
     If you don't die soon, I'm going to
     have to kill you.

                    MAN
Might be a minute, I'm getting there
though.

He keeps snorting. Lying down in the middle
of the street. Clumsy, spilling shit
everywhere.

                    GIRL 2
HELLO!?!??!!?!

                    MAN
Getting stabbed hurts so bad. I
didn't think it would hurt this
bad. I never would have hurt people
if I knew how bad it hurt. I'm a
changed man. Wow.
          (beat)
I'm lying. I'm lying about that.

A cell phone rings. Girl 2 turns around and
listens for the ringtone. It's coming out
of the man's pocket.

                    MAN
Oh shit.

Girl 2 walks over and runs his pockets for
his phone.

                    MAN
Hey, don't fuck with that.

She answers the phone.

               VOICE ON PHONE
          (v.o.)
Steve?

                         GIRL 2
        ...

                    VOICE ON PHONE
                      (v.o.)
    Steve? Is that you? We got him! We
    got the fucker, Steve! Pinned him
    down over on 4th. WE GOT HIM!!

She hangs up the phone and starts dialing
911.

                         GIRL 2
    Who are you.

                         STEVE
    Steven. Steve for short.

                         GIRL 2
    Hello? Hello—yes I need the police.
    I need police immediately. Yes—NO.
    I CAN'T HOLD. THE GUY IS HERE! I'VE
    FUCKING GOT HIM ON THE STREET, HIS
    NAME IS STEVEN!!

                         STEVE
    Steve.

Headlights turn on. A pick-up truck barrels
down the street.

                         GIRL 2
    AAGGGHHHHHHHHHH!

Girl 2 drops the phone and starts to move
out of the street.

The truck is going fast as hell, it hammers on the brakes.

It seems like the car will brake in time, but it slides a bit further. It misses Girl 2, but the front bumper collides directly with Steve's head. The car stops short of running him over, but the impact whips his head directly back into the concrete, killing him instantly.

> GIRL 1
>> (o.s.)
> STOP! THAT'S HER!

Girl 1 gets out of the car and runs over to Girl 2.

> GIRL 1
> Oh my god, are you ok?

> GIRL 2
> Yeah, I'm ok, listen, we need—

> GIRL 1
> We got him! You won't believe it, but I ran for help and found the group and. And they got him!

The Vigilante Leader and Vigilante 1 get out of the car. The Vigilante Leader is looking at a map on his phone.

> VIGILANTE LEADER
> On the app he's right here.

                    VIGILANTE 1
I'm looking—oh my god. Steve! He
must've got Steve!

The vigilantes gather around Steve.

                 VIGILANTE LEADER
God dammit. We got him, Steve. We
got him. You didn't die in vain.

                      GIRL 1
We got him.

Girl 1 hugs Girl 2.

                      GIRL 2
You got him? That's him! That
fucking guy is the rapist!

                    VIGILANTE 1
Who?

                      GIRL 2
FUCKING STEVE! He confessed! He
stabbed the whor—the fucking girl
we met earlier! That's the fucking
guy!

                    VIGILANTE 1
What are you talking about? Steve?
Steve's been working with us every
night to keep these streets safe.

                 VIGILANTE LEADER
Steve was a good man. A soldier.
He would've loved more than anyone
to put the cuffs on this sick fuck
himself.

                    GIRL 2
HE'S THE GUY. THIS IS THE GUY. I
DON'T KNOW WHO YOU GOT, BUT THIS IS
HIM.

                    GIRL 1
Hey, hey. This is crazy. I don't
know what's going on here. But they
got him. I saw it all happen. I ran
for help and found them pulling him
out of his Altima. Just like the
girl said. They caught him jacking
off in there.

                  VIGILANTE 1
We did.

                    GIRL 2
All of you need to listen to me.
I found her body. I tried to save
her. This guy—STEVE—pulled a knife
on me! He admitted to killing her.
He admitted to all of it!! He's the
fucking guy!!

                VIGILANTE LEADER
You're not listening. You're acting
crazy. It's over. We got him.

                  VIGILANTE 1
You need to calm down. We caught
him red-handed. Jacking off in his
Altima.

                VIGILANTE LEADER
Steven wasn't perfect but there's
no need to sully a good man's name.

                    GIRL 2
You didn't catch the 8ᵗʰ Street
Rapist. You caught some weirdo
jacking off in a car. Where is this
guy?

                  VIGILANTE 1
Truck.

Girl 2 goes to the truck. She looks in the
cab, then the truck bed. She moves a tarp
covering something in the back.

                    GIRL 2
Oh my god.

A man is lying in the truck bed. Handcuffed
and beaten to a pulp.

He's dead.

                 VIGILIANTE 1
We got him.

              VIGILANTE LEADER
Our streets are safe now. Think it's
time for you ladies to go home.

Vigilante 1 loads Steve's body into the
backseat.

                  VIGILANTE 1
I'd give you a ride, but we're a
bit full up now.

              VIGILANTE LEADER
You know, Steve used to be in charge
of walking women home. He loved to

do it. Would stay up all hours of
the night making sure women got home
safe. Well, nothing to be afraid of
now anyway. Have a good night.

The vigilantes drive off. Girl 2 is speechless.

                    GIRL 1
So. So, was that not him?

                    GIRL 2
No.

                    GIRL 1
That was just a guy jacking off in
a car.

                    GIRL 2
Yeah.

                    GIRL 1
Well. You got him then?

                    GIRL 2
She got him.

Girl 2 nods to the prostitute's corpse.

Still in the street.

                    GIRL 2
I don't even know her name.

                    GIRL 1
You know what she did. Who she was.
Names aren't that important.

                    GIRL 2
     They are.

Girl 2 sits down.

The sun is starting to rise.

                    GIRL 1
     It's pretty much morning. I could
     probably get an Uber or something
     now. Kind of over walking.

                    GIRL 2
     Sure. Whatever.

                    GIRL 1
     Was he even Estonian.

                    GIRL 2
     No. I don't think so.

                    GIRL 1
     Euuuhgh. When they pulled that guy
     out of his car he was speaking
     another language so I just assumed,
     Estonian right? What language do
     Estonians speak?

                    GIRL 2
     I have no idea.

                    GIRL 1
     Seven minutes. Amari in a black
     Prius.

                    GIRL 2
I think we have to become much
smarter than we are right now. All
of us. Everyone.

                    GIRL 1
Yeah, definitely. Like DuoLingo and
all that. Reading books instead of
timelines. Going to the park.

                    GIRL 2
Yeah. Maybe we need to go to the
park more. Read in the park.

                    GIRL 1
Where's the closest park.

                    GIRL 2
I don't know.

                              THE END.

10 Brief Interviews with Parents on the Experience of Watching Their Child Die

1. *"I didn't like it."*
    -Male, 62, Topeka, KS

2. *"I didn't like it."*
    -Female, 52, Corpus Christi, TX

3. *"I didn't like it."*
    -Female, 25, Hialeah, FL

4. *"I did not like it."*
    -Male, 29, Tulsa, OK

5. *"I didn't like it."*
    -Female, 37, Plano, TX

6. *"I would not do it again."*
    -Male, 34, Modesto, CA

7. *"Didn't like it."*
    -Male, 51, Scottsdale, AZ

8. *"I probably wouldn't do it again."*
    -Female, 45, Binghamton, NY

9. *"I didn't like it."*
    -Male, 38, Norfolk, VA

10. *"No thanks."*
    -Female, 47, Chicago, IL

2003 PRESS JUNKET - GARY COLE

INTERVIEWER: Four years of *The West Wing* and you seem to fit into the new season like a glove. How did you find your footing on season five of such a critically acclaimed show?

GARY COLE: It's pretty easy when Aaron [Sorkin] is writing your lines. [Gary laughs]. But truthfully, above and below the line I'm surrounded by such talent that it makes my job as easy as it can be.

INT: Did you feel any pressure joining midway into such a strong run? In the previous four seasons I don't think a single episode has premiered to less than 10 million viewers.

COLE: 10 Million, huh? Wow. Well, I try not to focus on the accolades. I've never felt the need to tailor a performance to fit something like that. I trust my director and the writers and if they're happy, then I'm happy. Whether it's in front of 10 people or 10 million I think I'll give the same performance every time.

INT: This is our first time meeting, but I have to say you seem incredibly well grounded for an actor as highly lauded as you are. I hope you don't take this the wrong way, but I've sat with some other talents and you don't exactly...

radiate? Like other actors. Do you think this helps you slip into your roles easier?

COLE: I don't seem like an actor to you?

INT: No, no no, not at all! I mean—

COLE: I'm kidding, I know what you mean. I'm not exactly Will Smith, right? I can still go into a mall and shop with no hassle and I promise you, I don't take it for granted.

INT: You go to malls a lot?

COLE: Yeah, I like to dress nice there. At the mall. I wear nice pants, shirt tucked in, sometimes even a suit. I'll wear something nice like that and I'll walk around for a while. See who's there. Who isn't. I like pretty girls. Pretty soon I'll find a girl and I'll follow her for a bit. Not too long, but just long enough to make sure she's not with too many people. It's easier if she's alone, but I'll still do it if she's with a friend or two. Anyway, after a few minutes I'll kind of jog up to her and grab her shoulder and say something like, "Hey, Steph!" The shoulder is good, but sometimes I'll grab her hand or even her waist. I decide in the moment. I try to use a different name every time, but I end up using "Steph" a lot. Once they turn around I let go quick and start to apologize, "Oh my god, I'm so sorry. I thought you were my friend Steph, I-I'm, so sorry." I stutter my apology to sell it more. Makes me seem more nervous and uncomfortable. They always buy it because I'm wearing nice clothes and I'm not that ugly. It wouldn't work if I was ugly or I dressed bad. I walk away embarrassed and they think I'm this awkward guy who made a mistake. I'll do this to two or three girls and then go home.

INT: So, it's a sexual thing? A compulsion?

COLE: At first, maybe yeah. Like a reaction to a sign that tells you not to touch something. You want to touch it because you know you can't. But pretty soon the rush of lying became much more intense than any touch. Lying right to their face. Because what are they gonna do? Call security and say I thought they were someone else? I barely even touched her. I made an honest mistake and there's no way they can prove I didn't. Plus I'm white.

INT: Do you find this helps at all with your process?

COLE: No.

SCRAPS

INT. BURGER KING - DAY

> WORKER
>
> What would you do if you were trapped on a desert island?

> CO-WORKER WITH SLIGHTLY MORE POWER BUT IS NOT A BOSS
>
> Die probably.

> WORKER
>
> Before that.

> CO-WORKER WSMPBINAB
>
> I'm the only survivor? Like *Castaway*?

> WORKER
>
> Yeah. Just you and I guess you get a bunch of random packages. That seems fair. Also I think it's *Cast Away*. Two words.

> CO-WORKER WSMPBINAB
>
> I haven't seen it.

                    WORKER
I haven't either.

              CO-WORKER WSMPBINAB
I think first thing I do is take
inventory.

                    WORKER
Classic.

              CO-WORKER WSMPBINAB
Open all the packages, see what's
useful, what's not. I actually
think I'd really enjoy that part. I
love opening presents.

                    WORKER
Who doesn't. Ok, so you've taken
inventory. What's next.

              CO-WORKER WSMPBINAB
Next is a toughie. I want to get
started on my shelter, but I have
to take care of the human aspect
and bury my fellow passengers.

                    WORKER
There's no passengers, it's just
packages on the plane.

              CO-WORKER WSMPBINAB
There's no way there's just
packages. I was flying a plane by
myself? Nobody flies a plane by
themself.

                    WORKER
In the movie I think it was just
packages.

               CO-WORKER WSMPBINAB
You haven't seen the movie.

                    WORKER
I feel like I would've heard about
it if there was a part in *Cast
Away* where he buries bodies or
something. It's usually just the
volley ball or the raft. I think
I've seen the part where he's on
the raft actually.

               CO-WORKER WSMPBINAB
Co-pilots man. Every pilot flies
with a co-pilot. There's gotta be
at least one body with me.

                    WORKER
Ok. I guess that sounds right.

               CO-WORKER WSMPBINAB
So I bury the body. I make a big
show of it too. Nice deep grave,
nothing shallow. Elegant tombstone.
Engraving might be too hard unless
I have like a chisel or something.
I would look for a unique rock
to mark it. Cover the grave with
leaves. Real big show. Gotta reduce
the temptation.

                    WORKER
Temptation?

                    CO-WORKER WSMPBINAB
Yeah. You make a big show of it and
you'll be fine. You really work on
that grave and make it something
you're proud of and you won't have
any issues later. Cuz you know...
        (beat)
If you just kick some sand on him
and cover him with a frond. Well,
we all know what happening man.

                      WORKER
What's a frond.

                    CO-WORKER WSMPBINAB
Sure, you're good for that day and
maybe one or two after. But three
days? You're pulling that frond off.
You know it, I know it. You dig a
nice grave though? No way you're
reversing all that hard work. All
that craftsmanship. That grave is
staying sealed.

                      WORKER
What are you talking about.

                    CO-WORKER WSMPBINAB
I'm fucking the body, man. Come on.
Everyone stranded on an island is
fucking the body at some point. I
don't want to, it's not high on
my list of shit I wanna do, but
after a few days I know I will. Big
show burial. Say a few words. Say
a prayer. That's why. You bury the
body **early** and **deep** so you won't
fuck it.

                    WORKER
I wouldn't fuck the body. I could
live to be 100 on that island and
that body would be as un-fucked as
it was on day one.

              CO-WORKER WSMPBINAB
You can say that all you want, but
you are not in a mental space where
you can truthfully answer that
question.

                    WORKER
I am actually.

              CO-WORKER WSMPBINAB
I believe that you believe that,
but it's impossible to account for
how things will change. I promise
you after 72 hours on that island
you will not be you. Go three days
without speaking to anyone. Go three
days without a meal. Go three days
without hope. If you live like an
animal for too long you are going
to become one.

                    WORKER
I've gone three days without
speaking to anyone. Three days is
not a lot of days. That's a long
weekend.

              CO-WORKER WSMPBINAB
Listen, man. Really listen to me.
You have lived your whole life under
the consequence and expectation of
others. That's not a bad thing.

You should be mindful of how your
actions affect other people. That's
crucial to being human. But things
are different on island time.
        (beat)
For the first time in your life
you will be faced with absolute
solitude. You will tell yourself
that someone is coming, but the
truth of the matter is that you
will never see another person and
most likely another person will
never see you. From the moment you
crash you are redacted. Your story
is erased. No one will ever know
what you did on that island. You
are no longer on Earth. You are in
purgatory. You are in *Grand Theft
Auto*. Are you really going to stand
there and tell me when you load
that game up you're stopping at red
lights? Better not deal with it.
Avoid it altogether. Bury the body
early and **deep**. You'll be glad you
did.

                WORKER
I think it's unfair to ask me what
I would do in a situation and then
when I give my answer you say that
it's impossible to answer because
I'm not in that situation.

            CO-WORKER WSMPBINAB
You should get back to work.

EXT. WOODS - NIGHT

> CRAZY SCOTT
> You can't get away, Stacy! You're all mine!

> STACY
> I'm not running anymore, Scott. You won't get away with this. You're crazy.

Crazy Scott lunges at Stacy and grabs her throat like a crazy person.

> CRAZY SCOTT
> I'll make you choke on those words!

Crazy Scott pins her up against a tree. He chokes her with both hands and raises her off the ground.

> STACY
> Choke on this you fucking Jew.

Stacy snaps a branch off the tree and **stabs** Crazy Scott in the neck. He dies terribly.

Stacy collapses to the ground and catches her breath.

It's finally over.

> DAVID
> Oh my god! Stacy, are you ok?

> STACY
> David. It's so good to see you.

                    DAVID
Is he...

                    STACY
It's over.

                    DAVID
I still can't believe it was Scott
this whole time.

                    STACY
I know. I didn't want to believe it
either. He was acting crazy.

                    DAVID
Still a week left of summer. Think
we have time to take that trip to
the lake?

                    STACY
Lake? Hahahaha. After this trip I
think I'm taking a **break** from the
great outdoors.

                    DAVID
Yeah.
        (beat)
So, I kind of heard you both before
I got here. Like I heard your voice
and started running, that's how I
found you. And did you call Scott
a Jew?

                    STACY
What?

                    DAVID
Like. I heard Scott yelling, that's
why I came running. And he was
yelling about how he was gonna kill
you and how he was gonna make you
choke, and then I heard you say,
"Choke on this you fucking Jew."

                    STACY
I don't know. He was choking me,
he was trying to kill me. I don't
remember what I said. It all
happened so fast.

                    DAVID
Yeah, totally. I get it, so much
trauma. And such a scary situation,
like I'm so glad you're ok.
        (beat)
But I was right there. And I heard
you say that—I heard you call him
a Jew.

                    STACY
I mean, maybe yeah. I don't know,
maybe I said that—

                    DAVID
A *fucking* Jew.

                    STACY
I was angry. He killed all of our
friends. Eight of us came on this
camping trip and we're all that's
left. He cut Monica's face off and
put it in my tent.

DAVID

So that's what you do when you're angry. You call someone a Jew.

STACY

What the fuck is wrong with you, David? He was fucking choking me—he was trying to **kill** me! Who cares what I said?

DAVID

So you did say it. Glad we could admit that... I'm just trying to understand **why** you said it. Do you use that word a lot?

STACY

You can say *Jew*. It's not a curse word. Scott's not even Jewish so I don't understand why you're freaking out—

DAVID

You know I'm Jewish right, Stacy?

STACY

Oh my god, David. You're half Jewish and you've never even been to Jewish church.

DAVID

I'm Jewish, Stacy. Half-Jewish is Jewish. It's called a synagogue and if you can't understand why it would be hurtful to me—your friend— to hear you talk like that then... you still have a lot of learning to do.

111

                    STACY
You celebrate Christmas! I've seen
a Christmas tree in your house! You
eat bacon!

                    DAVID
I was raised in an interfaith
household.

                    STACY
You know, you're right. You are
Jewish, David. You're acting pretty
fucking Jewish right now.

                    DAVID
Stacy!

                    STACY
I know you were hiding. We all did.
Once people started dying and you'd
be like, "Uhh, I'm gonna try and get
cell reception." We know you were
hiding in the tree trunk. Monica
saw you in there.

                    DAVID
I don't know what Monica thinks
she saw, but we all went through
a terrible experience. A terrible,
traumatic experience—

                    STACY
Fucking Anne Frank. Hiding in the
log while your friends die. What
were you writing in your diary in
there? "If Scott finds me in this
log it'll be 110 places I've been
kicked out of!" Fucking bug.

DAVID

Ok so there actually is a Jewish
thing with you.

INT. JAIL CELL - DAY

                    INMATE
So you wanna know what I did, huh?
Well I'll tell you, just so you
know I'm not in here for no funny
business. We're cellmates after all.
One thing you should know about me
is I love sports. Since I'm a kid
I love running around and kicking
and throwing balls. Don't matter,
soccer, basketball, football. If
it's outside I was playing it.
My favorite though... kickball.
Nothing like seeing a granny pitch
roll down the line and winding up a
massive boot to the moon. I think
it was so fun because it wasn't
really a real sport so you could
only play it at recess. No kickball
on TV, you know? Anyway, I loved
kicking that ball, but you get
older and suddenly there's a lot
less recess going on, right? You
wake up one day and realize you've
kicked your last ball. Depressing
stuff. Real depressing stuff. So one
day I'm hiking behind the Wal-Mart
and I see this kickball next to a
pile of trash. I probably haven't
seen a kickball in 15 years. Wide
open space behind the Wal-Mart and
I just know I've gotta blast this
thing. I scope the scene and it
looks like the coast is clear so
I get my two step line up, cock
my shit back, and BLAST my foot
through this motherfucker.

BUT FUCK! My foot hurts! The ball goes far, but not as far as it should and SHIT! My foot hurts! Feels like I just kicked a brick or something. So I look down and it's a fucking guy! Homeless guy sleeping in this pile of trash and he was using the ball as a pillow! Holy shit, I just kicked this guy full force in the dome. It was like an optical illusion. The ball was half deflated and he was using it as a pillow, but from the way I walked up I swear it looked just like a pile of trash next to a ball. Just crazy angles, you know? A truly insane angle. Any other angle and it would've been obvious it was a guy, but from my line, it didn't look like that. Not like a guy at all.

(coughs a bunch for like a minute)

Sorry, I'm real sick my body is shitty. Anyway, I look down and I got this guy good. He's bleeding bad out his head. Probably because of the kick. I get down and try to apologize for doing that and see if he's ok, but he's not ok. His eyes are open, but he is not there. What do you do? CPR, right? I get my hands on his chest and start doing CPR, but then I realize I don't know CPR and I'm just doing what I think is CPR. How long are you supposed to do it for? How hard? What exactly is it? I keep pushing on his chest, but he's making noises now and it's sounding like I'm hurting him even worse. Apparently if you don't know CPR you're not supposed to do it even if you're trying to save someone because it's negligence or something. They were dicks to me in court about that. Who sleeps with a ball for a pillow? Come on, man! So yeah, the guy dies, he does not live, what do you expect, I kicked the shit out of him. But he was not doing well to begin with. He was not surviving a kick to the head from anyone, least of all me who really blasted him. That should've counted for something, how sick he was to begin with. He could've died that day even if nobody kicked him! I just sped up the process a bit. I was in the wrong place at the wrong time, but I know what you're thinking, and I'm one step ahead of you, I completely agree. People that abuse or hurt the homeless, the houseless, those guys are sick. Those people are evil no doubt about it. But what about the thousands of innocent Americans that kill homeless people purely by accident? Surely you can't lump me in with those other freaks? I was just kicking a ball!

                    BIG Z
Ok playboy. I'm thinking in a couple
of minutes me, Roger, and another
guy named Roger are gonna rock your
holes.
                    ROGER
This guys a pedophile.

INT. LECTURE HALL - DAY

                    COLLEGE GUIDE
In college you will have an
opportunity to reinvent yourself.
A fresh start. You can be anyone.

                    LOSER
I will be a winner.

                    VIRGIN
I will be a ladies man.

            GUY WHO GOT MOLESTED
Yeah, ok, I've got an idea of who I
would like to be.

EXT. GOLF COURSE - DAY

                    JAY
First lesson's free, boys.

Jay hits the golf ball with his golf club
making it travel 224 yards.

                    SEAN
Not bad.

                    TERRY
Looks like 224 yards. Pretty good.

                    JAY
Gonna be a long one if you gotta
follow drives like that all day.
I'd start drinking now if I were
you.

                    TERRY
Way ahead of you.

                    SEAN
As long as I'm out of the office I
could hook shit for 18 and still
have a great day.

                    JAY
Speaking. Are you prepped for the
all hands on Thursday? I've been
waiting to get specs back from that
basement guy and he ducks all my
emails.

                    TERRY
Yeah, I'm good to go.

                         JAY
I think it's cuz I saw him watching
porn on his phone at lunch. Since
then he never responds to me. You'd
think he'd respond quicker because
I've got like a blackmail on him or
something, but nah, it's only made
shit worse.

                        SEAN
Let's not talk about work, man. I'm
not ready and I don't need any more
reminders about it.

                         JAY
What do you want to talk about then?

                        TERRY
I'll be right back, gonna piss real
quick.

Terry leaves to piss.

                        SEAN
That's such a weird thing to say.
Nobody asks, "What do you want to
talk about," they just start talking
about it. No good conversation has
sprung from, "What do you want to
talk about."

                         JAY
Ok, I can respect that. Give me a
minute then.
        (beat)
Do you think you could make Terry
cum?

                         120

                    SEAN
What?

                    JAY
Do you think you could make Terry
cum? Simple question. Not office
talk.

                    SEAN
No, that's a stupid fucking question.

                    JAY
Gun to your head, you couldn't do
it?

                    SEAN
Who would put a gun to my head and
say "make Terry cum."

                    JAY
Nobody, but that's not the point.
It's about limits. Stepping up to
the plate. Self-preservation.

                    SEAN
You're an idiot.

                    JAY
So, just to clarify. You're in a
life or death situation where your
only chance at survival is to make
Terry cum and you're dying.

                    SEAN
Yeah, I guess I'm dying.

                    JAY
Really? I never took you for the type
to give up like that. I thought you
were stronger to be honest. More of
a warrior. Guess I was wrong.

                    SEAN
It's a stupid fucking question,
man. It would never happen! What
do you want to hear? If your insane
fantasy ever did become real and I
really had no other option to live,
then yes, obviously I like living
and I would make Terry cum.

                    JAY
So you would.

                    SEAN
Yes, I fucking would.

                    JAY
But could you.

                    SEAN
I just said I would what more do
you want.

                    JAY
Yeah, you said you **would**. That's the
easy part. But **could you**. That's
the question. See, you're acting
like once you decide to make Terry
cum that it's a given. You're some
sex god that can make Terry cum at
your whim. What if you try to make
Terry cum and you can't.

SEAN

I obviously haven't thought about
this as much as you.

JAY

Have you made guys cum before?

SEAN

Obviously not.

JAY

See this is what I'm talking about.

SEAN

You can go back to office talk,
meetings, specs, whatever.

JAY

Just listen for a second and
respect the question. You're in
an unfamiliar position with the
highest stakes possible. You might
crack under pressure. Your technique
might be off. You've admitted you're
inexperienced too. A lot of guys
get to the majors and crack under
those bright lights. You think you
can shine?

SEAN

I'm not going to the majors, you
want me to jack a guy off.

JAY

So you would jack him off? That's
your plan? No mouth? Your life's
on the line and you're not going
straight to mouth?

123

                         SEAN
          Yeah, that's my plan.

                          JAY
          What if Terry can't cum from
          handjobs? He might need that mouth.

                         SEAN
          I do not care what Terry needs,
          man. Let's play golf.

Terry returns.

                         TERRY
          Yo.

                          JAY
          Terry, do you cum from handjobs?

                         TERRY
          Sometimes, but not usually. It's
          gotta be really wet. It's a whole
          thing.

                          JAY
          "Not usually," see this is what I'm
          talking about.

                         TERRY
          What are you talking about?

                         SEAN
          I'm done man.

                          JAY
          You talk a big game, but there's no
          way you could make him cum.

                    SEAN
I'm done.

                    JAY
You're pathetic.

                    TERRY
There's no way you could make me
cum.

                    SEAN
FINE, I WON'T JACK HIM OFF. I'LL
CUP HIS BALLS AND GIVE HIM SILLY
MOUTH UNTIL HE **POPS**. I'LL LOOK HIM
STRAIGHT IN THE EYES AND THROAT HIS
SHIT UNTIL I SPIT UP CUM OR VOMIT,
WHICHEVER COMES FIRST. I'LL BE HIS
LITTLE FUCKTOY AND HE CAN USE MY
MOUTH LIKE A PUSSY AND MY ASS LIKE
A MOUTH. WHATEVER PORNSTAR MOVES
IT TAKES TO ESCAPE YOUR RETARDED
HYPOTHETICALS, I'LL DO THEM.

Jay takes out a gun and points it at Sean.

Terry pulls his pants down fast.

                    JAY
Really. Wow. You would do that huh.
Pornstar moves. How about that.

EXT. PARK BENCH - DAY

> GUY 1
> I don't know. I don't think that's
> an issue. Like at all.

> GUY 2
> A problem then.

> GUY 1
> It's not a word choice thing. I'm
> not looking for a better synonym. I
> don't think it's a problem either.

> GUY 2
> Oh, then we do disagree because
> it absolutely is a problem and it
> needs solving.

> GUY 1
> What is she saying again?

> GUY 2
> She won't stop saying "You're not
> wrong."

> GUY 1
> "You're not wrong?"

> GUY 2
> Yeah. Like. Like we were out with
> her sister the other day. Getting
> breakfast. Her sister goes, "I
> don't know. I guess I would just
> have an easier time dating if all
> men weren't such idiots?" And then
> Alice, she puts her hand on mine and
> goes, "Well, *you're not wrong.*" She

can barely get the words out before she's cracking up. She thinks it's the funniest shit ever.

GUY 1
So you're pissed because she called you dumb.

GUY 2
No. Listen. I would love her even more if she'd just call me a retard or whatever, but she can't stop saying, "You're not wrong." She's addicted. It's like she heard it on Parks and Rec ten years ago and every time she says it she thinks she's fucking Leslie Knope. "You're not wrong." She's watching TV and some dude on SNL calls Trump some orange man bullshit and she looks at me, "Well...he's not wrong!" FUCK! Just say something else! Say nothing!

GUY 1
Ok. I get it. I still don't think it's that big of a deal, but I admit it could be a little bit annoying.

GUY 2
Thank you. Yes. It is annoying. That's all I'm asking for.

GUY 1
So what then. You ask her to stop saying it?

                    GUY 2
Can't just ask her. Then she'll
bring up some annoying thing I do
and put me under a microscope. I
can't take that. No way.

                    GUY 1
So you're living with it.

                    GUY 2
Yeah. Might start hitting her.

                    GUY 1
Hitting? Her?

                    GUY 2
Yeah.

                    GUY 1
I don't think that's right. You're
not supposed to hit your girlfriend.

                    GUY 2
Obviously. I know that. I agree in
theory. But think about this: What
if it works. What if I hit her and
she stops saying it.

                    GUY 1
I believe she might stop saying it
if you hit her, but that problem
will be replaced by a much bigger
one: You are now beating your
girlfriend.

                    GUY 2
My options are limited. I have
no other options. You know when
a doctor is like, "We can't cure
you. But we have an experimental
procedure that we'd otherwise never
try." This is a last ditch attempt.
If it works it works. This is my
experimental procedure. Hitting.

                    GUY 1
How.

                    GUY 2
How what?

                    GUY 1
You've put so much thought into the
justification. So how are you doing
it? Slapping her? Hitting her with
a belt? Pushing down the stairs?

                    GUY 2
Pushing her down the stairs? Are
you fucking insane? I don't know
what she'd have to do to get me
to push her down the stairs. No,
probably just like a slap? Slap her
up a bit.

                    GUY 1
So multiple slaps.

                    GUY 2
I mean, yeah. If the first one
doesn't take. Others will follow.

                    GUY 1
Considering you've never hit her
before, I imagine the first one will
take.

                    GUY 2
Yeah, probably you're right. So
it's a good idea? Hitting? You're
on board?

                    GUY 1
No.

                    GUY 2
Maybe I'll wait for her to say it
again and hide her shoes. Hope like
her unconscious brain connects the
two events somehow.

                    GUY 1
Yeah sure whatever that might do
it.

                    GUY 2
Shoes in the recycling bin. Cat
litter. Something like that. Keep
hitting in the back pocket for now.
Save it for a rainy day. I just
need a good alibi. Can't have it
getting back to me.

EXT. TOUR BUS - NIGHT

                    ARTIST
     If you wanna get on the tour bus
     you're gonna have to suck off my boy
     Rallo.

                    RALLO
     That's me.

                    ARTIST
     That's Rallo, the man you will be
     sucking off.

                    FAN
     I suck him off and I'm in?

                    ARTIST
     Yea.

                    FAN
     Just him?

                    ARTIST
     YEa.

                    FAN
     There won't be other guys?

                    ARTIST
     There might be other guys.

INT. FOOD TRUCK - DAY

                    CUSTOMER
          Can I have a chili cheese dog?

                    HOT DOG MAN
          Chili cheese. You want that with
          the mild or scorpion chili?

                    CUSTOMER
          I'll do the scorpion.

                    HOT DOG MAN
          Chili cheese and get the scorpion
          chili this bitch is tryna shit.

INT. COCKTAIL PARTY - NIGHT

TODD

Just met Michaela's new boyfriend.

MIKE

What's he like.

TODD

Don't know.

MIKE

Didn't you meet him?

TODD

Yeah, but not really I guess. He was trying to describe his job, but it was taking way too long and I kinda phased out. He was talking so much and I just had no idea what he was saying. He even had a neat little analogy ready to go to explain it because he must have to explain what his job is so often. He said that shit and I gave him a, "Ohh, I get it, I get it," but I didn't understand it at all. Something with insurance.

MIKE

Could you kill him?

TODD

(beat)

Yeah, I think so.

MIKE

Ok, I've got a read on him then.

                         TODD
I think I'm done meeting people. I
know enough people.

                         MIKE
You're not that old, I think you're
gonna have to keep meeting. You can
cut it off at like 80, maybe 75, but
until then you gotta keep meeting.

                         TODD
I can't wait that long.

                         MIKE
You talk to Racist Jeff yet?

                         TODD
There's a guy here named Racist
Jeff?

                         MIKE
Oh, you don't know RJ? You should
definitely meet him before you go.

                         TODD
He sounds racist.

                         MIKE
Nah, not at all actually. It's just
a joke. Couldn't be a nicer guy.

                         TODD
Really?

                         MIKE
No, not really he is racist a little
bit. But he is a nice guy, I wasn't
kidding about that.

                    TODD
So he is racist.

                    MIKE
Who isn't these days.

                    TODD
Me. You.

                    MIKE
Yeah. But still. Once you spend some
time with him you'll see what kind
of guy he is. Few months ago he took
all the accounting guys out fishing.
Hosted all of us on his boat. Just
out of nowhere. One day he's like,
"Let's go fishing my treat," and we
did it. Had a great time.

                    TODD
He took all the accounting guys?

                    MIKE
Well, almost all of them.

                    TODD
Didn't take Ja—

                    MIKE
Jamal was busy I think, couldn't
go. He had a car thing or something.

                    TODD
People call him RJ?

MIKE

Sometimes. He's just a fishing nut.
I think that's why he brought us.
One of those guys that loves fishing
and sharing it with people.

TODD

But there's some stuff he doesn't
love right. Like certain races of
people.

MIKE

You're focusing on the least
interesting part about this guy. He
took all of us, like six people, on
a fishing trip. Out of nowhere. It
was a Friday and he was like, "Who
wants to go fishing. I will handle
all of the logistics. You just say
yes and we're going fishing." He
made it happen man. I was ready to
go home and all of a sudden I'm on
a fishing trip. He took care of all
the meals too.

TODD

You had a good time?

MIKE

Everybody had a good time. You know
how sometimes on a group trip there
can be heads butting or someone feels
excluded or something. Nothing like
that at all. Couldn't have gone
smoother. Everyone caught a fish.

136

                    TODD

Was he...racist..at all? During the
trip?

                    MIKE

Racist? Come on man, we were too
busy catching bass to be racist.
Waking up around 11 and casting a
line with a cold one. That's the
thing too, you know how sometimes
people get up early on trips? They
have nothing to do because people
are waking up at different times.
Never happened. We were sleeping
in every day. Everybody on the same
page. Just a good time man, that's
all it was.

                    TODD

So Racist Jeff was not racist at all
during the fishing trip.

                    MIKE

No. Not at all. I mean, not overtly.
Obviously that's RJ so there's gonna
be a little bit here and there,
but it wasn't anything crazy. You
could've missed it if you weren't
paying attention.

                    TODD

But you were paying attention. And
he was being racist.

                    MIKE

You've latched onto the smallest
part of his personality and you-
you're making this big deal out of

                    137

nothing! He's just a guy. Is he perfect? No, but who is? You've never met him and you haven't even given him a shot. Here, I'm grabbing him. You're gonna see.
(to other group)
Hey, Jeff! Jeff! RJ! Come over here!

Racist Jeff comes over.

RACIST JEFF
Mike! My man how are you.

MIKE
Great, great man! I wanted you to meet Todd. One of my oldest friends and I was just telling him about that fishing trip.

RACIST JEFF
Nice to meet you.

TODD
Yeah.

RACIST JEFF
What a trip that was. Hey, if you've got a second I'd love to tell you about this next trip I'm planning. Two days on Clear Lake, gonna be beautiful. Let me just take a big sip of water first. I need to clear my throat because I'm planning on saying the n-word later and I don't want anything to go wrong.

MIKE
Ahh man come on.

INT. OPERATING THEATER - DAY

Dave is splayed flat on his back on the operating table. His hands and feet rest on four disconnected smaller tables. His arms are rotated 180 degrees so his palms are down and his elbow joints face upwards. Hundreds of eager spectators watch from above.

> DAVE
> Ladies and gentleman! My esteemed colleagues! I am DAVE! WELCOME! TO THE EXPERIMENT!

Four men walk in carrying 100lb kettle bells. They each position themselves next to one of Dave's joints. Two knees and two elbows. They raise their kettle bells up in unison.

> DAVE
> BEGIN!

The men drop their kettlebells and break Dave's knees and elbows backwards.

> DAVE
> AGGHHHHHHH! FUCKKK!!!! AGGHHHHH!
> OH MY GOOODDDD OH MY GOOD.
> AGHAHHDHGHHHHHHHHHHHHHHHHHHH!!!
> HUHHH !!HUHHHGHH!! HUAHHHHHHHH.
> OH MYY FUUCKING GGOD!!!!!!
> AGGGGHHHHHAFHDHHHHHHHHHH!!!
> SHHAHHHHHHAHGHGHHHHHHHHH!
> FUCKK!!!!!!!!!! FUCKKKK!!!!!!
> HUHHHHHHHHHH! HEWUUUUUHHHH
> HUEHUHHH!!!!! SHFUCKKK!!!! FUUCK
> OH MYY GOOOD!!!!!! FUCK!!! I
> NEED HELP!!!!!! IN NEEED FUCKKING

HELPP!!!!! OH MY GOD!!!! HUEHHEHGHH
HUEHHHEH!! HUHEHGHHH! MY FUCKING
LENGS!!!!! SHMYYY MY MY LEEEGGGS ARE
GONE!!!! MY LEEEGGGS AARE **FUUCKEDD**!!!!
SOOMEEBOODY!!!! AHAHGHGHHH!!!!
SOMEBODY!!! HELP ME!!!!!!
HZZHUUUUU HZZUUUU HZZAAUUUUU!!!
OOH NOOOOOOOO!!!! OH NOOOOO!!!!!
NNNNNOOOOOOO!!!!!!!!!!OOO!!!!
NOOOOOOOOOOOOOOOOOOOOOOOOOOO
OO!!!!! NOOOO! HZZZEELELEPPPPPPPP
M V X E E E E E E E E E ! ! ! ! ! ! ! ! !
PUDZLEEAASSSSEE PLEASSEEEEE
PLEAASSEEEEEEE!!!!!! PZLEEASZEEEE
G H G O O O O O D D D D D D ! ! ! ! ! !
GOOODDDD!!!!! OOOOZOZZHHHHHHH MYYY
GDOOGOOODDDDDD!!!! MMZMOOOOMMMM!!
IGHHHIIIIIIIIII NNEEENNEEEDDDD
MHHHYYYYYYYYY MAOOHMMMMMMMMM!!!!!
F F F F U U C C C C F U C K K K K K K ! ! ! ! ! ! ! !
H H E U E U U H H Z H Z Z Z
H U E H U E U H Z H Z Z Z J H H S S H S H
H U Z H E E H Z H Z H Z H H ! ! ! ! !
A G G R H G H H H ! ! ! ! ! ! ! !
AGHGHGHHHHRHRRHHH!! I CAAANNTT
MOVEE IT!!! IGHIHHHH CAAANNNTT
MZHOVVEEE MYYEHHH LEGGGSSS AAHHHTT
ALLLLLLL!!!!!!!!!!!!!!!!!!!!!
HUHHHHH HUHHHHHHZZZZ SHUHZZZZZZ!!!
OK OK OK OKOKOKOKOK IEHMM GONNAAA
TRYH THOOOOOO MOVES MAHHYYYY
AHRRMM!!! FUCCCCCUKKKKKKK!! I I I
I II I CANTTTTTT I CAAANHHNNNTTT
MOVEE ANNYTHFING!!! NOOOOOO!!!!!!
NOOOOO!!!!! NO!!!!!! NOOOOOOOO!!!!
NOO!!!!!NNNNNOOO!!!!!!!!!!! MY
EXPERIMENT IS A DISASTER!!!!!!!!!!!

INT. PSYCHIC OFFICE - DAY

>   PSYCHIC
>   The pathway is open, what would you
>   like to say to your dead son?

>   FATHER
>   Hello.

INT. DEBATE HALL - NIGHT

                    MODERATOR
The challenging candidate will have
two minutes to address the topic,
then the incumbent will have two
minutes to respond. The first topic
is foreign policy. Begin.

                CHALLENGING CANDIDATE
If you elect me I will crush
Panama. I will raze their pathetic
countryside and entomb its history
in a graveyard of ash. I will put
their children in chains, their
women in brothels, and their men in
coffins. The collective remembrance
of this sad state will fade into
a false memory after my campaign
is completed. Their history, their
culture, their spirit, all reduced
to cinder in my war's wake. A new
holocaust. A justified genocide
and the American people will
crown me their king for it. I'll
stand anointed on a mass grave, a
necropolis of my own making, and
the world will cheer.

                    MODERATOR
Thank you. Mr. President, you have
two minutes for your rebuttal.

                    PRESIDENT
I will also crush Panama.

INT. HIGH SCHOOL CAFETERIA - DAY

>   ALLISON
> I still can't believe Jet asked you
> out.

>   TARA
> I'm in shock. I'm shocked. Like,
> what? He just came up to me at my
> locker? And asked me out?

>   ALLISON
> It's that skirt. I told you Saturday
> if you wore that skirt it was over—

>   TARA
> I almost didn't wear it.

>   ALLISON
> No because why did you walk in first
> period with your ass out and he
> couldn't wait until second to talk
> to you.

>   TARA
> Stoooopppp, my ass was not out.

>   ALLISON
> I saw the skirt Tara, it was fully
> out. The skirt was skirting.

>   TARA
> Wellllll... Maybe a little out.

>   ALLISON
> So, what are you gonna wear for
> your date?

                    TARA
Cut an inch off this and wear it
again?

                  ALLISON
You are so unserious.

                    TARA
I don't know, we have three days so
I could Prime something.

                  ALLISON
Go through my closet tonight, take
whatever. It's Friday, right?

                    TARA
Yeah, after the game.

                  ALLISON
Oh my god, I forgot. Game night?
He's definitely gonna be expecting
something after they win. You know
he only does anal right?

                    TARA
Yeah—wait. What?

                  ALLISON
Jet only does anal.

                    TARA
What do you mean? Like he doesn't
have regular sex?

                  ALLISON
Well, he does have regular sex.
But regular to him is anal. So not
really.

                     144

                    TARA
Shut up. You're fucking with me.
How do you know this?

                  ALLISON
How do you not know this? That's
like Jet's whole thing. Stacy
hooked up with him over the summer
when they were both upstate. That's
why she started this year in the
wheelchair.

                    TARA
What the fuck. You're joking. Stacy
was not in a wheelchair.

                  ALLISON
Ok yeah, she wasn't in a wheelchair,
but she was definitely with Jet. And
Jet only does anal. I can't believe
you didn't know that. Omg lol.

                    TARA
What does this actually mean?
Nobody "only does anal." Like if
I'm in his car and we're making out
he's just gonna be like, "Let's do
anal."

                  ALLISON
No, he won't do anything like that.

                    TARA
So what then?

                  ALLISON
No, I mean he literally only does
anal. He doesn't kiss, he doesn't

hug. Definitely doesn't make out.
He's not gonna hold your hand or
even like feel you up or anything.
He only does anal.

                  TARA
That's... what? What?! How does he
do that?

                ALLISON
Won state as a freshman. Had D1
offers sophomore year. He can do
whatever he wants. And all he wants
to do is...

                  TARA
Don't you think that's. Like...

                ALLISON
What?

                  TARA
...Gay? Doing only anal sounds
super gay.

                ALLISON
Don't be homophobic, he doesn't
fuck guys, Tara.

                  TARA
But. Only anal. No kissing. It
doesn't feel very straight to me.

                ALLISON
If you don't want to go out with
Jet, don't go out with him. There's
plenty of other girls in this school

who would die to have a chance with him. Like me. Oh my god here he comes.

                    JET
Yo.

                    TARA
Hey, Jet.

                    ALLISON
Hey.

                    JET
Friday.

                    TARA
Yeah. Definitely.

                    JET
Later.

                    ALLISON
Whore.

                    TARA
Shut up.

                    ALLISON
Didn't know you were into gay guys?

                    TARA
Shut up....Have you ever?
     (whispers)
Done it? It doesn't hurt, does it?

                    ALLISON
It's gonna feel like you're shitting

and there's a good chance you
actually do.

                    TARA
There's no way. No way. I can't.

                  ALLISON
Bloody too.

                    TARA
I need to talk to Jet. There's no
real proof, right? This is just
what you heard? What you heard from
someone who heard from someone who
heard from someone? This is a rumor
that got way out of control and
now girls two high schools over say
shit like, "Jet only does anal,"
and we treat it as gospel.

                  ALLISON
Ok, yes, it is something I heard
or whatever. But what do you
actually know about Jet? This is
what we know. Jet threw for 5,800
yards as a freshman and rushed
for another 2,000. 90 Touchdowns,
six interceptions. 78% completion
percentage. Since he first put on
shoulder pads Jet has not lost a
game. Ever. In his entire life.
Adults talk to this 17 year old
like he's their big brother. Every
time he steps out on the field he is
stepping into a dream that he has
total control over. For 48 minutes
he is closer to God than any of us
ever will be. Now how do you think

that personality transfers to the bedroom? Huh? You think anyone has ever told Jet, "No?" Sure, you know what? Maybe someone has told him no, but do you think for one fucking second Jet believed them? He doesn't know what that word means. He doesn't have to.

                    TARA
So what, he's gonna rape me? Is that what you're saying?

                    ALLISON
No, that's not what I'm saying. But if he did he would still start next Friday.

                    TARA
I feel sick.

                    ALLISON
Good. In the presence of God a man should feel unlike himself.

                    TARA
He just texted me.

                    ALLISON
Probably telling you to start training your hole tonight.

                    TARA
He said "gurmp."

                    ALLISON
What?

                    TARA

He texted me "gurmp." Oh wait. He
texted again. "ment 2 send dat to
som1 else."

                  ALLISON

Gurmp?

                    TARA

Yeah.

                  ALLISON

What else did he say?

                    TARA

He just said "gurmp." That's it.

                  ALLISON

Gurmp.

                    TARA

What does that mean? And why did he
mean to send that to someone else?
Does that mean something to someone
else?

                  ALLISON

Forget the god thing, you should
bring some plastic keys you can
shake in case he gets too riled up.

                    TARA

He texted me gurmp.

INT. BAR - NIGHT

                    SHMULI
You know what I love about being
sick? Sneezing in the shower. It's
like a free sneeze because you don't
need any tissues to clean it up.
You can just let the snot go and
the water gets it. Normally when
you're sick you're sneezing a lot so
you're going through more tissues
than usual and if a box of tissues
cost three dollars and it has 160
tissues then you're spending almost
two pennies per sneeze. Every time
you sneeze, poof, two pennies gone.
But a sneeze in the shower cost
nothing. It's free. If my nose is
really stuffed up I try to save it
for the shower because I know I'll
be saving more money if I do it
that way.

                    MICHAEL
You can't say stuff like that,
Shmuli. Not with a name like that.

EXT. DESERT - NIGHT

                    MOBSTER
When you borrow money from Jimmy
The Goop, you pay it back. Or else.
          (cocks gun)
Jimmy pays you back.

                    WELCHER
Please. Fellas. I know I fucked up,
but, I'm gonna pay. I'm gonna pay
youse back! I just need a couple
more days!

                    JIMMY THE GOOP
Two weeks is what you had. Two weeks
and you bring me this.

Jimmy The Goop throws a small amount of
money into the dirt.

                    WELCHER
It's all I got I swear! I just need
a few more days to get some things
rolling and I'll have the money.
All ten g's ya gotta believe me!

                    MOBSTER
Let me do em, boss.

                    WELCHER
I GOT KIDS, JIMMY! I SWEAR ON THEIR
LIVES I'LL GET YOU THE MONEY. I'LL
GET YOU 20 G'S YOU GIVE ME ONE MORE
CHANCE.

                    JIMMY THE GOOP
I want you to look at this.

Jimmy The Goop pulls out a bullet.

> JIMMY THE GOOP
> .45 ACP. Hollow point. Not your
> wife. Not your kids. Not your dick.
> This is gonna be the last thing you
> ever fuckin see.

The Mobster hands Jimmy The Goop his pistol.
Jimmy chambers the cartridge.

> WELCHER
> JIMMY. JIMMY. JIMMY THE GOOP, I'M
> BEGGING YOU. HOW'M I GONNA PAY YOU
> BACK WHEN I'M DEAD? HUH??? DON'T
> YOU WANT THE MONEY BACK?

> JIMMY THE GOOP
> Don't you get it? You didn't borrow
> 10 g's. I paid you 10 g's so I
> could do this.

Jimmy The Goop presses the barrel to the
Welcher's forehead.

> WELCHER
> NO. NO! JIMMY NO! JIMMY THE GOOP
> NO!!!!!!!!!!

> MOBSTER
> Look! Little man pissed himself!

> JIMMY THE GOOP
> You know what. You wanted mercy.
> Here's mercy. I'll give you a
> minute to clean yourself up so you
> don't meet Peter with piss all over
> yourself.

                    WELCHER
I didn't piss myself.

                    MOBSTER
This man pissed himself.

                    WELCHER
Look, I'm scared. I'll admit that.
I don't wanna die. But I didn't
piss myself.

                 JIMMY THE GOOP
I can see that you pissed yourself.
You got piss on your pants.

                    WELCHER
I don't have piss on my pants.

                    MOBSTER
You peed on the inside of your pants
and we can see it on the outside.

                    WELCHER
I didn't piss myself.

                 JIMMY THE GOOP
What's this then.

Jimmy The Goop points to the piss.

                    MOBSTER
That's piss.

                    WELCHER
No it's not.

JIMMY THE GOOP
So there is something on your pants
then?

WELCHER
Yeah. It's wet from the ground. It's
cold out here and I'm on the ground
and a wet spot from the ground got
on me.

MOBSTER
That is pee.

JIMMY THE GOOP
The pattern looks like the pattern
piss would make.

WELCHER
It's not. I can prove it. Smell it.
It doesn't smell like pee.

MOBSTER
I'm not smelling it.

JIMMY THE GOOP
We don't need to smell it, that's
piss. The burden of proof is on
you. If you can prove it you can
prove it, but you can't cuz that's
piss.

WELCHER
I can prove it.

MOBSTER
How.

                    WELCHER
Well. If I did piss myself would you
agree that I couldn't pee again?

                  JIMMY THE GOOP
. . .

                    MOBSTER
He could have only peed half and was
saving the other half for later.

                    WELCHER
Why would I save pee for later.

                  JIMMY THE GOOP
Ok. If you stand up and piss yourself
right now. We'll both admit that
you did not pee yourself.

                    WELCHER
Ok. It's just.

                  JIMMY THE GOOP
What.

                    WELCHER
I'm a little worried that both of
you know that I didn't piss myself
and this whole thing is a ruse to
get me to piss myself for real.
It's kind of a lose/lose for me to
piss myself to prove that I didn't
piss myself. Either way I'm going
to end up pissing myself.

                  JIMMY THE GOOP
You offered to piss yourself. This
was your idea.

MOBSTER

Make him pull his dick out so we can see the pee leave the hole.

WELCHER

Yeah, but it's not like you couldn't have planned this. I feel like a rat in a maze that you designed.

JIMMY THE GOOP
(cocks gun)

You pull your dick out right now and pee, I won't kill you.

MOBSTER

Let me see ya piece.

JIMMY THE GOOP

You can pee outside your pants. Piss for your life.

WELCHER

This is too much pressure. I'm sorry, but there's no way I can pull my dick out and pee in front of you under these circumstances. I know I can physically pee. I promise you that. I have pee locked and ready to go. But mentally... I need to at least turn away from you to get it going. I can't do it with you watching.

JIMMY THE GOOP

We need to see it.

MOBSTER

Show me that worm, trick.

                    WELCHER
Let me just turn around. I'll spin
180 degrees and keep a wide stance.
You can watch through my legs and
see the piss.

                    MOBSTER
He could be faking it with spit and
we'd have no idea.

                    WELCHER
Spit wouldn't look like piss I
wouldn't try that. They'd look
different you could tell the
difference.

                JIMMY THE GOOP
You can spin 130 degrees and keep
your head slightly to the left. We'll
be right outside your peripheral.
You won't be able to see us, but we
will have a thin line of sight to
your cock.

                    WELCHER
Even if you're on the edge of my
peripheral I don't know if I can
do it.

                JIMMY THE GOOP
You get 130 degrees and 60 seconds.
Go.

The Welcher turns 132 degrees.

                    WELCHER
Ok. Ok. Just. Relax.

The Mobster starts playing some pocket pool.

>   MOBSTER
>   Let's see what you got.

>   JIMMY THE GOOP
>   Fifty. Fourty-nine.

>   WELCHER
>   Don't count. That's fucking me up.
>   Just. Let me do this.
>   (beat)
>   Ok. Ok. Ok.

The Welcher closes his eyes and tilts his head back. He's in the zone now. We hear the faint sounds of a river. He runs his thumb back and forth across the base of his cock. The river gets louder and louder. We're approaching the edge. A waterfall can be heard in the distance. We're almost there!

BANG!

The bullet goes straight through The Welcher's brain. He collapses and Jimmy The Goop holsters the gun.

>   JIMMY THE GOOP
>   Check em.

The Mobster pulls the Welcher's pants down and puts his cock in his mouth. He starts sucking his soft dick with deep slow pulls like he's trying to siphon gas.

After four sucks he coughs and pulls the dick out of mouth. He spits out a mouthful of piss. The Welcher's dick is peeing.

                    JIMMY THE GOOP
          How about that.

2014 PRESS JUNKET - REESE WITHERSPOON

REESE WITHERSPOON: Ask me any question. Any math question go ahead.

INTERVIEWER: Ok. What's 17 times 156?

WITHERSPOON: Easy, 2,494.

INT: Wow, that's amazing. I don't know if that's right though. One second. Ok, I'm looking it up and that's not right.

WITHERSPOON: Well, I still arrived at that answer fairly quickly so you've got to give me some credit there.

SPORTS

"Grief Game" Strategy

In a must-win situation the best possible strategy is to kill a star player's family member to induce a "grief game." A grief game is a game preceded by a dramatic family death where the affected player simply cannot lose, lest he desecrate the memory of the deceased loved one.

Ideally your target player has *at least* four close family members so you have enough deaths to spread out over the course of a playoff run. Obviously, the effectiveness of this strategy hinges on the strength of the player's familial ties. An athlete who grew up as an anti-social orphan might not have as many bonds to break as one who grew up in a loving home.

One possible implementation of this approach would be to save four family members (EX: mom, dad, sister, grandpa) for one specific seven game series. This way you can guarantee the four necessary wins by killing one relative before every game. It's possible the overall grief may become too strong by game four, but most coaches believe this strategy would net you at least three strong wins.

It's important to note that this game plan becomes less effective as the familial relationship becomes more distant. Dead parents and siblings produce the best games, while the death of a distant cousin or irritating uncle may not even faze the targeted party.

Dead children can be a double-edged sword. Their death may be so powerful that they overwhelm the player completely. When Colts center Ryan Kelly's daughter was delivered as a stillbirth in December of 2021, Kelly did not play for the next two weeks. However, on November 12th, 2017 when Marquise Goodwin's child was delivered still-born he went on to play the Giants that same day. Goodwin had an 83-yard touchdown catch that would propel the 49ers to their first win of the season.

The death of a child is too emotionally complex to guarantee results. Most professional coaches would not recommend killing a player's child unless you had already killed off all of their parents and siblings. At that point you might consider killing a child as a last resort, but do so at your own risk.

"Grief Game" - References

• **6/16/96 - Seattle SuperSonics 75 - 87 Chicago Bulls**
In 1993 Michael Jordan's father was murdered, he would retire from basketball that same year. Three years later Jordan returns to the NBA and win his fourth NBA championship on Father's Day, putting up 22/9/7/2 over Seattle.

• **11/20/02 - West Forsyth High School**
Chris Paul scores 61 points five days after his Grandfather is beaten to death. One point for each year of his Grandfather's life.

• **12/22/03 - Green Bay Packers 41 - 7 Oakland Raiders**
Brett Favre throws for 399 yards and 4 touchdowns the day after his father dies suddenly of a heart attack.

• **5/11/14 - Pittsburgh Penguins 1 - 3 New York Rangers**
Martin St. Louis scores a goal on Mother's Day, three days after his mother died from a heart attack. In the previous nine playoff games Martin had not scored a goal at all. This win would force a game seven, eventually completing the Rangers 3-1 series comeback against Pittsburgh.

• **4/9/17 - Minnesota Timberwolves 109 - 110 LA Lakers**
De'Angelo Russell goes for 16/4/4/3 including the game winning buzzer beating three after finding out his grandma had died that same morning.

• **5/2/17 - Washington Wizards 119 - 129 Boston Celtics**
Isaiah Thomas scores 53 points (20 in the 4th quarter) on his sister's birthday two weeks after she died in a car crash. Celtics take a 2-0 lead in the playoff series.

• **10/3/24 - New York Mets 4 - 2 Milwaukee Brewers**
Two strikes on and down 2-0 at the top of the ninth inning, Brandon Nimmo holds strong and gets a base hit. This hit moves Lindor from first to third and sets up Alonso's 3-run game winning homer. One hour before the game Nimmo was informed his grandmother had died.

• **10/8/24 - Philadelphia Phillies 2 - 7 New York Mets**
Pitcher Sean Manaea throws seven innings and holds Philadelphia to one run after learning his aunt passed away that morning. Manaea had six strikeouts, propelling the Mets to a lead in a playoff series they would win (3-1).

Important to note this is not a guarantee, see below.

• **10/13/13 - Carolina Panthers 35 - 10 Minnesota Vikings**
Adrian Peterson puts up 62 rushing yards, 21 receiving yards, one fumble, and zero touchdowns in a staggering home loss to the Panthers two days after his infant son was killed by his ex's boyfriend.

Fantasy Football Punishments

-You come last in my fantasy league you have to blow up a building

-You come last in my fantasy league you're getting fucked out

-You come last in my fantasy league we're making you take out a loan

-You come last in my fantasy league we're killing you and making it look like a suicide

-You come last in my fantasy league we're feeding you glass through a feeding tube

-You come last in my fantasy league we're giving you Sophie's choice

-You come last in my fantasy league we're putting metal in you

-You come last in my fantasy league we're making you hang out with a guy that likes soccer

-You come last in my fantasy league you're losing your incisors

-You come last in my fantasy league we're mutilating your wife

-You come last in my fantasy league we're making you invest in a restaurant

-You come last in my fantasy league we're giving your pet a serious health condition

-You come last in my fantasy league we're gonna find your breaking point

-You come last in my fantasy league we're making you discuss race science in a public forum

-You come last in my fantasy league we're switching your right eye with your left eye

-You come last in my fantasy league we're putting crazy glue in your penis hole and jacking your shit real good

If they want to actually end racism they are going to have to write it much bigger in the end zone so everyone in the stadium can read it.

Shell Game Strategy - Basketball

The ultimate basketball team is made up of 15 players. They are all 6'8" or within 1-2 inches of that height. They all have similar builds. They all have similar facial features. They are all bald. They are all the same ethnicity. They all wear the same socks, shoes, and accessories every game. They all have no tattoos. They're all ambidextrous. They all have the same last name.

The idea behind playing this lineup is other teams have no immediate way of identifying who each player is. The star point guard looks exactly the same as the back up center. The three point specialist looks exactly like the interior slasher. The perennial all star is an identical double for the 15th spot bench warmer. The fast paced play of basketball will render all split-second reads useless. During player introductions 15 guys named "John Johnson" are announced as they come running out of the tunnel.

Imagine forcing a point guard left when that's really a left-dominant slashing shooting guard. Imagine trapping a center only for him to effortlessly pass out of it because that's the point guard. All inbound plays will be complete chaos. How can the defense identify the shooter during a breakout?

One potential problem with the Shell Game Strategy is each player must have a unique number. This is their only defining characteristic. It's not perfect, but a viable solution is to have all numbers be as similarly confusing as possible, EX: One player has 88, one has 89, one has 99, one has 98, etc.

The other team will know on paper who each man is, but during the heat of the game it will be much more difficult to identify who is 88 and who is 89. Additionally, a player's number is only visible from the back which limits potential identification time to mostly during transition. As stamina fades and mental capacities are drained it will be near impossible for defenders to assess who is who.

The only way this strategy fails is if any of the players are not that good at basketball so obviously the caveat is they all have to be generational players and shoot close to 60%. Then they will never lose.

Poker Tips

-If I am trying to get a bluff through I will tell my opponent that if they call me I'll kill myself right there at the table.

-Some players will be better than you. A quick way to close the skill gap is to cheat. The only drawback to cheating is getting caught. Avoid getting caught at all costs.

-Lie to your friends. Tell them you bought in for $300 when you bought in for $280. They are your friends so they won't be expecting you to lie to them.

-The best possible starting hand is "Pocket Rockets" (two black aces). Play anything else and you are motherfucked.

-The worst possible starting hand is "The Chinese Pair" (two red 2s). Play this if you don't care if your kids get braces.

-Beginners may get confused that some of the cards have numbers (2, 4, 9), while others use letters (J, Q, A). A helpful memory trick is to envision the jack as the "11", the queen as the "12", etc. You don't have kings, you have a pair of 13s.

-If you lose money at the table there is plenty of opportunity to get it back from weaker players later in the parking lot.

-If you win $58 in a home game and then lose $2,465 in a casino you are still up $58 because it's not good to think about how much money you are losing at the casino.

-Really do not think about how much money you are losing at the casino.

1994 PRESS JUNKET - TOM HANKS

TOM HANKS: Hey. Good morning. Good morning. Hey there. How are you? Oh! Hey, good morning.

INTERVIEWER: Doing great, thanks for taking the time to be here.

HANKS: Oh, no problem. Hey Rodg, how are you?

INT: Feels like you know everyone here already?

HANKS: Hollywood Reporter? I'm alright with faces. Did the same press run for *Philadelphia* in December. I've known Roger since *Big*. I don't believe I know you though, I think it was Haley last time?

INT: Wow, you really do know everyone. I trained under Haley. She's in New York right now, so I got the chance to fill in for her. Tracy.

HANKS: Tracy, I'm Tom. Great to meet you.

INT: Do you ever feel a bit silly introducing yourself? Especially at a presser for a movie you star in? There's a *Forrest Gump* poster right behind you.

HANKS: [Tom turns around to look at the poster and laughs] Uhh, maybe a bit? When you go over it like that yeah, but in the moment it's different. I think it's important not to assume anything. Before I'm Forrest or Beckett, I like people to know that I'm Tom.

INT: Of course. Well, it's a pleasure to meet you Tom.

HANKS: Likewise Tracy. Well, go for it! Let's talk about *Forrest Gump* before someone from Paramount comes down here with a gun! Pow! Pow!

INT: [Tracy laughs] Oh my god, yep, right away. Ok. Filming in Georgia I heard you developed a bit of a taste for okra? And that taste went as far as to be called an "obsession" by some of the crew. Can you tell me how you fell in love with Georgia's southern cuisine?

HANKS: Pow! Wow. Do you ever think about what you would do if someone came in here with a gun for real? Like what if someone came in here with a gun and made all of us have sex.

INT: Oh. Um. I-I'm not sure. Are you serious?

HANKS: Like, let's say a crazy insane guy comes in here with a gun. What, there's like 9 or 10 people in here? He makes all of us pair up and fuck. What would you do?

INT: He comes in with a gun and wants to rape us.

HANKS: No, no. He wants all of us to have sex with each

other. He's not involved in the sex. He's more of a conductor than a participant.

INT: I. I would fight back, I guess.

HANKS: Yeah, of course. But he's got a gun right? And he's not afraid to use it. I think if you try to fight back it could get violent. Let's say someone does stand up to him and the gun gets used. Someone has been hurt or god forbid, killed. He's threatening more violence unless his demands are met. What do you do?

INT: What do I do? I don't know how to answer this.

HANKS: If you don't—if we all don't—comply with his demands. He'll kill everyone.

INT: I call the police, I pray for help, I don't know.

HANKS: He's got all of our phones. He took all of our phones when he first came in and nobody can hear us we're totally isolated.

INT: I don't know.

HANKS: You have no options. You have to do it.

INT: Then yeah. I guess I—

HANKS: You have sex with someone, yeah me too I would

do it too. Obviously I do it. He's got a gun! At least he's not making us do it with him you know. It could be a lot worse.

INT: We've only got 10, 15 minutes here and I need to get some questions in about *Forrest Gump*.

HANKS: So who would you pick.

INT: For what.

HANKS: If someone came in with a gun and made us have sex with each other. Who in the room would you pair up with?

INT: I don't know. I can't answer that.

HANKS: Oh, obviously. You don't have to answer out loud. I get it these are your co-workers. You don't have to answer. But in your head. Go ahead and answer in your head. Because I know who I would pair up with. [Tom looks around the room] If someone came in here with a gun and that happened.

INT: I'd like to stop talking about this.

HANKS: It's making you uncomfortable? Oh for sure. We can stop... get back to the movie.

INT: Great. Thank you.

HANKS: It's not happening for real, you know that right? Nobody's going to come in here with a gun and do that. Make us—or anybody else—fuck. Just a little thought experiment. Something I was thinking about.

INT: I know. I know it's not happening for real.

HANKS: Because sometimes you see a girl. You see a girl and you're attracted to her and you just want to fuck. In a totally binary way. Yes or no. Instant reaction. You see something beautiful and you want it and that's it.

INT: ...

HANKS: But the girl doesn't always want you back, right? And that's it. That's life. I'm not a freak, I'm not a sicko. That's where it ends. It doesn't even begin. But you still think, right? What if. What if we were the last two people on earth. What if someone came in with a gun. What if we had no choice.

INT: Aren't you married?

HANKS: I would be gentle about it. I would be scared too if someone used a gun and forced us. I would comfort her. I would make it as easy as I could. I would tear up and apologize and say "I'm so sorry, but we have to do this." I'd follow her lead. But I'm worried I would be less scared. I'm worried that the girl would stop it if she could, but if I had the power to stop it... I don't know what I would do.

INT: What the fuck is wrong with you.

HANKS: Nothing? Maybe something. I hope nothing.

INT: I don't know what to do now.

HANKS: Did you know I'm probably going to win an Oscar for *Forrest Gump*? Anyone else would get in trouble for pretending to be a retarded guy and they're going to give me an award because I was so good at it.

1999 PRESS JUNKET - SALMA HAYEK

INTERVIEWER: That's Salma Hayek as Serendipity. *Dogma* opening this weekend in Los Angeles, November 12th. Thank you again and I hope you had a fantastic time with us at Access today.

SALMA HAYEK: Of course, always. Thank you, I hope you enjoy the movie.

INT: I'll be first in line. New York is opening the same weekend and I heard Kevin and the gang will be attending that premiere. How do you choose between the two? Do you try to do both?

HAYEK: One premiere is more than enough for me. I would love to be in New York with the rest of the cast, but I'm committed to another event here in LA.

INT: Oh my god of course. I know all about your charity work. We still have a few minutes, do you want to speak to that?

HAYEK: I don't know if it'll make the cut, but I'll never turn down an opportunity to talk about something I care about.

INT: I promise you it will. I'll make sure of it.

HAYEK: Well, I've been involved with the Special Olympics for quite some time and there are some preliminary events going on this weekend in Los Angeles! I'll be helping out with the athletes and trying my best to help raise awareness for the 2001 winter games in Anchorage.

INT: I can guarantee you this piece will help with that. How long have you been involved with the Special Olympics?

HAYEK: In January it will be five years.

INT: That's amazing. Your entire career practically. What drew you to the organization?

HAYEK: Oh, it's impossible to point to just one thing. The energy, the feeling of all the athletes working together is too powerful to stay away from. The strength of everyone involved is so inspiring it quickly became an event I look forward to every year.

INT: What are some of your favorite memories from your work? You ever try your own hand in any of the events? Give the 100-yard dash a shot?

HAYEK: Oh no, of course not. I'm regular so it wouldn't be fair. There was this one athlete named Derrick that always stuck with me. You know those toy candy phones? Derrick had one and was always using it. Pretending he was on a phone call you know? Just talking and talking all the time. He would hear other people talk on the phone and mimic their cadence, their phrases. Just be walking around saying stuff like, "Oh yeah. Ok. Yeah. Yeah. I'll see if I can make it. I'll SEE if I can make it." Anyway one day I was helping monitor sign-ups when Derrick and his coach walked in. Derrick is on his toy phone, talking nonsense as usual, while his coach filled out the sign-up sheet. Then the coach gets a call on his real phone and tells me he has to step out. He asks me if I can watch Derrick for a second.

INT: Are you comfortable with a request like that? Being responsible for a complete stranger?

HAYEK: I've known Derrick for a few years, he's no stranger. So the coach leaves and I try to talk with Derrick, but he's locked in. Totally focused on his pretend phone call. No interest in me at all. It's like I'm not even there.

INT: I find that hard to believe.

HAYEK: It's true! He just loves to talk on the phone. I'm a nobody to him which I actually kind of appreciate. So I go back to my work and he keeps up his conversation. Going on and on and on. Occasionally he'll end a call and chew on the phone for a bit. Then right back to another work call. This goes on for a few minutes and then.... there's silence. I look up. Now besides Derrick's developmental problems, he's also got a host of physical issues. You wouldn't need to see him eating his toy phone to know something is off with him. He's legally blind so his eyes are always scrunched up like someone is shining a flashlight in his face. I notice the silence and look up and... he's staring right at me. Because of his condition even if he's talking to you he's usually never looking at you so I was startled. He's looking right at me and then... his face relaxes. It changes. He fully opens his eyes and shifts his face out of what it has always looked like. His posture corrects. He doesn't say anything to me, but he doesn't need to. A smirk creeps into his face. A smile I've never seen before. He's been pretending to be disabled this whole time. It's unclear why he's sharing this with me, but it feels like a threat.

INT: Oh my god. That's crazy. What happened next?

HAYEK: Derrick's coach came back and they left. He went back to being his usual self. The scariest part is I can't remember if this is something that actually happened or something that I'm scared might happen. I'm losing my grip. The more time I spend with the athletes the further I slip out of reality. I'm worried they're all pretending now.

INT: So, wait a second. That didn't happen?

HAYEK: I don't know. I don't know if it did.

INT: Wow. Well, thank you for sharing. I'm looking forward to the movie, hope you have a great day.

[Salma doesn't answer. She stares out the window for three minutes and then leaves]

FOR IMMEDIATE RELEASE -

Procter & Gamble has issued a global warning to all customers who have purchased the following products between October 2022 and December 2024: Head & Shoulders Classic Clean Anti-Dandruff Shampoo, Head & Shoulders Charcoal Anti-Dandruff Shampoo, Head & Shoulders Coconut Anti-Dandruff Shampoo, Head & Shoulders Clinical Dandruff Defense Sensitive Shampoo, Head & Shoulders Aloe Vera 2 In 1 Dandruff Shampoo and Conditioner, Head & Shoulders Avocado Oil 2 In 1 Dandruff Shampoo and Conditioner, Head & Shoulders Clinical Strength Dry Scalp Rescue Shampoo.

These products contain active ingredients of piroctone olamine and selenium disulfide. These chemical compounds are safe to apply to the scalp, but recent independent health studies have uncovered that direct exposure of the aforementioned products may cause unintended lasting damage to alternative parts of the body.

It is unequivocally stated here and reinforced by the FDA, Procter & Gamble, Head & Shoulders, and all supervising scientists/health experts that under no circumstances should any consumer jack off using Head & Shoulders Anti-Dandruff Shampoo or any of it's aromatic/clinical strength variants.

No matter how horny or alone you are, **do not jack off with Head & Shoulders Anti-Dandruff Shampoo**. Proceeding with this course of action may cause shampoo to enter your penis hole which will induce an acute burning sensation during urination. If you were using a lot of shampoo and jacking off extra soapy this irritation may last for 1-3 days. It will also hurt when you cum so please don't fucking jack off again even if you're home alone and trying to get the most mileage possible out of an empty house. It will really really hurt if you do that.

The burning sensation during urination can be so intense that you may try to hold your piss back in an attempt to reduce the amount of urinations per day. Do not do this. It will only compound the coagulated selenium in your urethra. Frequent urinations will cleanse your tube and make it so you can piss and jack off again without agonizing pain.

If the pain of urination is too intense it can be mitigated by filling a cup with warm water, submerging your cock, and then peeing underwater. This can soothe painful urinations during the body's natural cleaning process of the urethra. Please remember to not overfill the cup with water because it needs to hold room for the piss too.

It may be better to use a mug or wide basin because if the cup is too tall your soft penis may not be long enough to be submerged while still leaving enough empty space for urine. **Make sure you leave enough room for the pee** because it will be a mess if your dick is on fire and you don't react to the overflowing piss cup and it spills out all over the kitchen floor because you decided to do this in the kitchen because that's where the microwave you used to warm up the water is and you don't own a mop or have any paper towels.

Customers may contact the P&G U.S. help line by calling (877)-435-7733 Monday-Friday between the hours of 9:00 AM EST and 4:30 PM EST.

This company announcement is conducted on behalf of independent studies organized and vetted by the U.S. Food and Drug Administration.

Proctor & Gamble

26 Things You Should NEVER
Say to Your Boss

1. fuck you boss

2. Suck my dick boss

3. See you later in the parking lot boss, I'm going to kill you there

4. Your mouth looks like a great place for my fist boss

5. I hate this job and you, the boss who gave it to me

6. Hello boss, it's me your employee. Prepare to die

7. I got a gun in my bag

8. I'm planning on harming your pet tonight boss

9. You got elephant ears

10. the k-slur

11. Your daughter looks like she would be easily traumatized boss

12. When I drive to work I pray that a truck driver dozes off and rear ends me at a red light, sending my carseat headrest directly into the back of my neck, paralyzing me and rendering me incapable of ever driving here to work for you again

13. Have a sip of your coffee boss, you look thirsty and I have poisoned it

14. Is it ok if this project waits until Thursday, my daughter has a soccer game

15. Is the circus in town? Because it seems that a clown has just walked into the office. I'm talking about you boss

16. Good morning boss, please kill yourself

17. Prepare to be destroyed

18. In four more days the waiting period for my handgun will be completed. I hope that is not bad news for anyone who works here

19. Your wife will be my slave in this life and the next boss

20. I have rigged a nail bomb to explode in your home tonight boss

21. I have broken the law and paid an assassin $40,000 to perform the illegal crime of murdering you boss

22. Can I leave early

23. I could kill you and nothing in our universe would change boss

24. Give me your car boss. If you refuse I will take it by force

25. Hey boss, I just bought a spring assisted blade online and when Fedex brings it to me I am going to be springing it open over and over all day at the office and if someone surprises me or suddenly asks me to stay late on Friday, I might just become so startled that there is a really bad accident for someone who is not me

26. [While holding a katana] Say your prayers ho

7TH GRADE DIARY

September 11th

I am the dumbest kid in the smart math class. I've been in the smart math class since 3rd grade and it was always easy, but now I'm in 7th grade, and they're trying to teach me algebra and this shit is fucked.

I thought I had math under control. I have a strong grasp on numbers. Forty-five, forty-six, etc. Even fractions and decimals—I'm pretty good at those too. They're just small numbers. But yesterday, Mr. Helena drew an X on the whiteboard and it was over for me.

September 14th

Math class sucks. It's the only class I walk slow to. Mr. Helena asks us questions, but I'll never raise my hand because I don't get it. I think I could get it, but I'm not getting nearly enough time to.

The other kids raise their hands fast so they must get it pretty quick, but I have a feeling that even if they didn't get it they would still raise their hands because they love

189

raising their hands so much.

It's a good thing I'm in the smart math class, because if I was any dumber I might internalize my failure and become jealous of the regular kids until I snap and shoot up the school. They are so lucky I'm smart enough to realize how dumb I am. I'll just keep going to class and staring at the clock for now.

September 18th

People are saying that Amanda in 8th grade gave a freshman head, so I am going to have to figure out what that means.

Amanda is in my math class even though she's in 8th grade which means she is kind of dumb for her grade, but she seems to understand algebra much more than me so what the fuck. This won't be good for me socially if it gets out that the girl who does head is smarter than me.

September 19th

I finally figured out how to use X in math. Then today Mr. Helena drew a Y on the board, and I started to freak out. Thank god there is one kid in class dumber than me and he is much louder about it.

Miles might be as dumb as me in math, but I am much better at hiding it. When a problem is on the board, I look at it, chew my eraser, and write things down. To most of the class I bet it looks like I know what's going on.

When Miles doesn't get something, he raises his hand and yells, "I DON'T GET IT," before he even gets called on. He does a great job at shifting attention away from me.

Even at my lowest points in math class, I am grateful for Miles' social and mental retardation.

September 22nd

People are now saying that Amanda actually had sex with a freshman and he was wearing a condom, but it fell off and got lost in her pussy. I guess this is something I should be worried about. Good to know that this can happen and I will watch out for it. Head is a blowjob too.

October 2nd

Three boys in my grade have to take math in the basement. They're even dumber than the regular kids like Miles. You'd think they'd get made fun of for being so dumb they have to learn underground, but nobody says anything. Probably because they can all throw a football across the whole yard.

October 4th

Took a small bite of pizza at lunch and got called gay for it. I got caught taking a gay bite. Felt terrible the rest of the day.

October 5th

I called another kid gay at lunch. I felt like god.

October 10th

In the schoolyard this morning, we were talking and Ethan said he had a dream about me. In his dream I was a hammer and I kept jumping around saying, "I'm a tool!

I'm a tool! I'm a big tool!"

He got some laughs from that, so I had to fire back. I told him, "I had a dream about you too Ethan. You were gay and sucking your Dad's dick."

This felt like a fatal blow when I said it, but then Ethan said, "You were dreaming about me sucking my Dad's dick?" and it was pretty much over for me right there. Kind of dug my own grave, but you have to take those shots sometimes. At least I went down swinging.

October 13th

Every day before the bell rings, Ethan asks me if I had any more wet dreams about him fucking his Dad and everyone laughs. Don't see this ending anytime soon. Why did I say that.

October 16th

Jason jumped into a pile of leaves and broke his neck yesterday. Since then, Ethan has not mentioned my fictitious gay dreams. Yesterday I asked God for a break which is weird because I never ask God for anything because he's not real, but now I'm a little worried that God is real and he broke Jason's neck for me. If he did, then I have a very powerful ally on my side. Ethan would be unwise to cross me again.

October 18th

There's a picture going around on Facebook of Jason in the hospital. His arm is in a sling, and he's got a big neck brace on. Miles said if you have to stay at the hospital for more than three days you're allowed to ask the nurse to jack you off. I don't think this is true, but everyone agrees that there must be some type of system in place.

October 25th

Jason came back to school today. He didn't break his neck, only his collar bone. We asked him if the nurses jacked him off and he said no.

October 27th

Jade, the goth girl in 8th grade, is talking about killing herself on Halloween. She's not in school today because her parents found out she's doing a sacrifice suicide and got in big trouble. At least that's what I heard from some other kids, I've never talked to Jade.

I hope she doesn't do it because she's in my top five hottest girls and I need her to at least accept my friend request before she kills herself. Ethan said she has a bikini picture on there.

October 30th

Jade didn't come to school today either.

October 31st

So, Jade is fine. She didn't come to school today again, but she posted a crazy long status about how kids at our school are nosy and fake. Her dad is really sick and that's why she missed days. She's pissed that half the school is saying she killed herself while she's been at the hospital with her family.

I found this out when Ethan sent me a screenshot of her status. She still hasn't accepted my friend request. Maybe if I change my profile picture and send it again she'll think I'm someone else and accept it. Maybe she's just busy with her dead dad and they don't have good internet in the hospital. I need a plan.

November 1st

During assembly today, Miles got caught sitting with his legs crossed—which is how girls sit. Ethan said only girls sit like that because if a guy tried to sit like that it would hurt his penis so that must mean Miles has a small dick. I usually don't sit like that, so my dick is probably normal sized.

November 2nd

I looked up average penis sizes online and it turns out I have a small dick. Not good.

November 3rd

I forgot to delete the search history of me looking up average penis sizes, so I was stressing all morning about Mom using the computer and thinking I'm gay. I calmed down at lunch when I realized Mom doesn't know what search history is and I'm not gay.

November 6th

In language arts today we had to write a book review of our favorite book. I asked if I could write about Mad Magazine, but it's not a book so I couldn't.

Jason's arm is still in a sling from his accident so he can't write. This is bullshit. Whenever we have writing exercises he gets out of it. Ethan said the real reason he wasn't writing a book review is because he's retarded and has never read a book.

He said it kind of quiet, but Jason yelled back, "You're fucking retarded," and Ms. Montgomery definitely heard it then. She hates it when people say curses, but it really got to her this time. She made everyone put their pencils down and told us a story about the power of words.

She said she has a sister and one day when they were kids they were fighting in the back seat of a car. Calling each other names and stuff. Ms. Montgomery started tearing up and said she regrets it every day, but she called her sister, *banana face*. Her sister was so sad about this that she wigged out, opened the door, and jumped out of the moving car. She almost died.

This was supposed to make Ethan not say *retarded* I guess, but this was the funniest story I've ever heard. I couldn't stop laughing. "Banana face" isn't even a real curse word. What is wrong with her sister.

November 9th

Every time we're in language arts or see Ms. Montgomery in the hallway, someone says "banana face" under their breath and we all crack up. I think she's ignoring it. If it wasn't the funniest thing I've ever heard, I would feel bad.

November 14th

There's a Chinese girl in my class named Zhu (like the place with the animals). She looks Chinese, but speaks regular. She's one of the smartest girls in school and she plays saxophone too.

Today in the cafeteria she put a cookie in the toaster and it got stuck and caught on fire. They had to evacuate the cafeteria and now older kids are calling her *Toasta Girl*. It doesn't matter how smart you are.

November 17th

Saying "banana face" has finally become less funny. Nothing lasts forever, but Miles has especially been annoying about it. At lunch he was singing "banana face" over and over like an opera singer. He was using a banana like a microphone too. It's like he doesn't even understand why it's funny. It's not a song.

November 20th

At recess I saw an 8th grader playing football with an Under Armour skull cap and he looked so cool. I need an Under Armour skull cap for when I play football.

November 21st

The caps on Gatorade bottles should not be screwed down so tight. I got a yellow one with lunch today, and I couldn't get the top off. I tried the first time and didn't get it. I tried a second time and still didn't get it. The third time, I put my shirt around the cap for more grip and really ripped it. Still nothing.

At this point I was worried someone at the lunch table was watching me and counting how many times I failed to unscrew the cap, so I put the Gatorade down and went back to my sandwich. After a few bites of that I deemed enough time had passed to try the Gatorade again. I tried a fourth time, and it didn't come off. I took my hand off and shook it out to reset my fingers. Fifth try, and it didn't budge.

At this point I looked up and saw Ethan watching me. I don't know how much of my Gatorade struggle he saw, but thank god I got it off on the sixth try. He didn't say anything, so I have to imagine he only saw two of my attempts. Two tries is safe for opening bottles. You can't make fun of someone for taking two tries. Anything after that would have been fair game to unload on me.

If I get Gatorade again I will have to open it in the bathroom or at least prep it there so I can easily open it in public. People can't know how hard it is for me to open Gatorades.

November 28th

Everyone is in trouble. Someone drew a swastika in the second floor boys bathroom and the teachers are freaking out about it. We had an assembly where the whole school had to listen to a speech about hate and how you should never draw a swastika and all of that type of stuff.

Funny enough, the black kids are way more mad about this than the Jews. People have been writing the n-word in the bathroom for years and we've never had an assembly about it. Maybe because they say it themselves all the time but still, it does seem like bullshit.

None of the Jews seem to really care except for this one annoying Jewish girl Sarah. She cares a lot and is making sure everyone knows how much she cares. I hate Sarah.

November 29th

The school is being extra protective over the bathrooms now. They can't put cameras in them obviously, but they are definitely making the janitors hang out near the bathrooms way more than usual. Then, once you leave the bathroom, the janitor goes in and checks to make sure you didn't do anything racist in there.

One of the janitors is Miles' dad and people call him a pedophile because of his weird mustache and glasses. You can imagine how much more he is being called a pedophile now that his job is to spy on kids in the bathroom.

December 1st

I'm almost positive that David drew the swastika. He's Jewish and I've seen him drawing swastikas in his history textbook before. He usually says some funny shit during assemblies, but he was totally quiet during the swastika one. Ethan brought it up first and said he was acting like Anne Frank because he wasn't making any noise. Everyone laughed, but I had to look up who Anne Frank was later.

December 13th

I thought things were chilling out because Miles' dad is following us into the bathroom less, but I was so wrong.

We had computers class today and we were supposed to do presentations on the websites we made about our hobbies. Ethan did one on lacrosse, Miles did one on metal music, then it was Sarah's turn.

Sarah didn't have anything. Not even one page.

Mr. Aguilar asked why she wasn't prepared, and she said she was so stressed out from the swastika in the bathroom that she hasn't had time to do any of her school work. This is total bullshit because the swastika thing was like three weeks ago. Sarah is only mad because she's an A student in every class except for computers. She's a girl, so she barely knows how to set an away message.

Any other teacher would have failed her, but Mr. Aguilar is so nice. He didn't even yell at her. He told Sarah to see him after class to talk about it, but she started milking it super hard and even started crying. She was saying how Mr. Aguilar could never understand what it's like as a Jewish person to see a symbol of hate.

Mr. Aguilar is Mexican—or at least speaks Spanish—so he probably does know what that's like. He also drives the shittiest mini-van in the parking lot (Ethan calls it a "beaner bus") and Sarah gets dropped off in a Mercedes.

None of that matters to Sarah though, so she started sobbing and saying the holocaust is the worst thing to ever happen in world history and seeing that symbol (how could she see it, it was in the boy's bathroom??!) made her feel unsafe at school.

Mr. Aguilar only feels comfortable talking about HTML so it seemed like he was gonna give her a pass until Marcus raised his hand. Marcus is the only black kid in computers class, so I knew whatever he was gonna say was gonna be great.

Marcus didn't even wait to get called on. We all knew what he was gonna say before he said it, but he still let it rip. "What about slavery? That was way worse than the holocaust."

Once he got that off, I knew class was pretty much over. There's no way we can do websites when Sarah is crying about trains and Marcus is yelling about boats. It's tough because computers is one of my favorite classes. It would have been much better to have this debate in math, but I'll take what I can get.

The gist of Marcus' argument was that slavery lasted for over 500 years and the holocaust was only like five so slavery was worse. Sarah said you can't compare gas chambers to working outside.

It seemed like Marcus was getting the upper hand when he said Jews were pretty much fine after the holocaust, but black people were still poor and hated after slavery.

Sarah lost it and screamed, "That's because you're easy to hate!" Then she left.

Both made great points; I don't know who's right. Sarah and Marcus are both in my history class, so hopefully they'll pick it back up there.

Nobody else did a presentation on their hobby website. Mr. Aguilar was too stressed and said we'd finish the rest of them on Thursday. I was actually excited to do mine. It was about Halo 2.

December 14th

I went into the bathroom and someone wrote "banana face" next to where the swastika used to be. I laughed so hard I threw up. It's funny again.

TO: ABEBE@PETSMART.COM

FROM: JHURLEY@PETSMART.COM

SUBJ: Workplace Vocabulary Reminder

BODY: Armando,
When referencing potential pets, please refrain from saying that they can bring "pure pleasure" to the customers. I have heard you use this phrase multiple times this week in reference to the hamsters and guinea pigs.

You may say the animals are "cute" or "fun," but please do not reference "pleasure" in any form when talking about them. I want to believe this is a misunderstanding, please give me no reason to think otherwise.

Thank you,
Joseph Hurley

Shift Manager
PetSmart #2235

2022 PRESS JUNKET - JOHN LEGUIZAMO

INTERVIEWER: John, you've had such a storied career. Film, television, broadway. Actor, producer, comedian. One man shows. Emmys and Tonys. I would call you a multi-hyphenate, but even that is underselling your talent. How did you piece it all together?

JOHN LEGUIZAMO: Oh, thank you. I wish I had a better answer, but it's just the result of thirty years of hard work. I've been blessed to build a tight professional circle that does their best to get me in these positions. I'd be nowhere without managers, agents, casting directors. I'm very fortunate people still pick up when I call.

INT: I promise your hard work does not go unnoticed. When you look back at your career is there one specific moment that jumps out at you? A memory of movie magic?

LEGUIZAMO: Oh man. Pointing to just one would have the terrible effect of leaving so many other deserving ones out. You know what, one memory does jump out. More of a feeling than a specific memory, but every time I get to sit in a theater and experience the project I've been working on with a real audience is magical. Lights go down and it's quiet. I find myself listening to the audience more than the movie. You can hear every laugh, every gasp, every reaction. I can't get enough of that.

INT: Great answer. Would you say you go to the theater a lot then? You prefer that over the home viewing experience?

LEGUIZAMO: Of course, nothing beats the theater. It's untouchable. Not even a question.

INT: What makes the perfect theater visit for you?

LEGUIZAMO: Popcorn, coke, no one on either side of me. Total silence. Total darkness. That's bliss. You know I almost had a perfect visit the other week, but I lost my keys during the movie! God that was awful. It would've been one thing to finish the movie and then realize my keys were gone. That would've been fine. At least I could've enjoyed the movie, but the instant I realized my keys were gone I couldn't focus. I'm touching my pocket and wondering where I could've left them. I figure the keys probably fell out of my pocket and they slipped out the back of the chair so they're on the ground somewhere. I was wearing sweatpants and shit always falls out of those pockets. There's no interior grip on sweatpants pockets. You sit down anywhere in those things and your pockets are getting dumped. I wanted to be comfy in the theater so I wore them. You have to get the ones with zipper pockets.

INT: That makes sense.

LEGUIZAMO: So I try to swipe my hand under the seat, just trying to feel for the keys, but I don't feel shit. They must have fallen so far back. I can already tell I'm gonna have to get out of my seat and get on my hands and knees to reach far back enough to find them. I try to ignore the keys and focus on the movie, but I can't. The keys are burning a hole in my head now. I can't relax and watch the movie until I know where my keys are. I don't even know how long the movie is. Usually I look that up before I go, but this time I didn't.

INT: So what did you do?

LEGUIZAMO: I sucked it up and got down there. Fully out of my seat. I'm down there on my knees and I try looking around, but I can't see shit. It's dark as hell in that theater because the scene playing takes place at night. There's no light coming off the screen at all. I get back in my seat and I gotta wait for a scene in daylight to check again. Like five minutes go by and nothing. I'm not even watching the movie anymore, just waiting for daylight. This whole fucking movie takes place at nighttime. I can't wait any longer so I go back down on my knees into the darkness. I still can't see shit, but I just reach further. I'm up to my shoulder now under the seat, reaching for something that might not even be there. I can feel some popcorn that the guy behind me must've spilled. I keep reaching, my head is practically under the seat now and then I feel it. The serrated edge of my car keys. Thank god, right?

INT: You found them? That must've been a huge relief.

LEGUIZAMO: I can just fit my middle finger in the key ring and I'm about to drag them back when I hear the guy behind me groan and a wad of cum hits my hand. I've never been cummed on before, but it hit my hand with more force than I ever would have expected. I thought it would be like a snowflake landing on you, but it's much more powerful. Maybe because he was aiming down, but I could feel the impact. I drag back my keys and I wipe my hand on the seat next to me. Had to go to the bathroom to really clean it though. Couldn't finish the movie.

INT: What movie was it?

LEGUIZAMO: I have no idea. Can't remember. Too much was going on.

ONLY 10% OF PEOPLE CAN READ THIS !

Cngroalutiaos! Fi yuo cna raed tihs yuo aer a prat fo a slecet lckuy guorp fo poelpe taht hvae avdnaecd mnids. A rseeacrh sudty ta Hrvarad Uvniesitry cndoectud yb ginesues fnuod uot taht olny ohter ginseues cna raed stenneces wittren lkie tihs. Is't ipmotrnat to be on tlesvieoin. As lnog as teh fsirt adn lsat lteter fo a wrod aer in teh rgiht pacle, a gneuis mnid is albe to raed teh wrod! Yuo suohld do smeohnitg in pbluic taht gtes yuo on tveseilion. Lokos lkie crocert sepilnlg si nto as iprmotnat as ew tuoghht it wsa! Tkae taht thcaeres! I rmeebemr wehn oru teachres siad we wulod neevr be giensues. Bhloed su nwo, wr'ee giesnues atefr all. Is't lagel to onw a gnu in all fftiy sattes adn yuo cna do smehtoing wtih it to gte on tlseieiovn. If yuo can raed tihs aazmnig masesge, sahre it to fnid ohter ginesues!

2024 PRESS JUNKET - KATE MCKINNON

KATE MCKINNON: They need to add a huge fat fuck to SNL. 470lbs and he's breathing heavy through every sketch. That would make me watch again. Even when he's off camera you can hear him breathing. They bring him into every scene with a forklift and it makes the backing up sound even if it's driving forward.

NIGHTMARES

There is no need to do any further analysis into any of this. Dreams are most likely all random and have no bearing on real life.

All of these dreams were recorded between 2021 and 2024.

NIGHTMARE METER
1 - Fine
2 - Less fine
3 - Bad
4 - Very bad
5 - Very very bad.

Construction

I am taking a tour of a massive construction site. The building's frame stretches far into the sky, probably an apartment complex of some kind. In the center is a flat open area for a courtyard. Scaffolding covers every inch of the worksite. Workers cut wooden beams and fill the air with sawdust. The soundscape is polluted with power tools. If I didn't have a guide I'm certain I could get lost here.

The foreman shows me around and tells me things I can't remember, gradually leading me higher and higher up into the structure. At one point he boasts about the view and I look out into the city. I can see a park. It's far away.

Both of us are wearing those yellow construction hard hats even though the rest of our clothes don't match. He's wearing a suit and I can't remember what I was wearing, but it didn't match. Those hard hats always make you look stupid unless you have the perfect head because they sit real tall on your skull. Neither of us have the perfect head and we both look stupid.

As we ascend higher and higher the building becomes less finished. There are fewer workers populating the space, fewer walls put up. Soon we've reached the top most point you can walk to. There's still an outline of the building above us, but to go any higher you'd have to be on the scaffolding outside. I look out and appreciate the beautiful view. I think I'd have much less fun looking down, so I don't.

There is a rumbling. The uniform sounds of work below us are disrupted and I can hear power tools switch off.

The support beams start to dance like I'm on acid. I hear loud talking and then louder shouting from the workers. A much larger rumbling sounds and now the foreman and I both feel the floor shift beneath us. It might be an earthquake or a structural failure, but something is fucked.

CRASH

Walls fall. Everything is shaking so I drop to my knees to have more points of contact with the floor. Beams crumble, chunks of wood and iron rain down around us. I shake the fear for a second and try to crawl back to the stairs but they're gone. The stairs we walked up have collapsed and taken chunks of the floors below down with them. No exit. We can't go back the way we came. The building continues to sway and the foreman tells me what we have to do. Jump.

There is a square hole in the floor about 10'x10'. I look down and the drop seems suicidal. Three stories at least, maybe more. Things always look higher when you're looking down, but I'm sure if I jumped face first from this height I would die. The drop is tall enough to kill you for sure, but if you land on your legs and roll or something, you might be ok (ok being not dead).

The building is shaking more and more now. The foreman tells me this is our only option. The building is collapsing and if we don't jump we are going to die up here. There is no more time for debate, we are jumping. I grip the edge and lower myself down into the hole, hoping to drop from the smallest height possible. He wishes me luck, I let go, and I fall.

I'm in the hospital. My legs are majorly fucked. Thick casts on both of them and my left arm/shoulder is strung up too. Moving anything hurts, looking anywhere hurts. I don't feel happy to be alive, but I am.

I'm alone. I can't move my neck much, but I hear wheels rolling on the hospital floor. They're getting closer.

The door opens and one of those TV carts is rolled in. It rolls in further and I see who's pushing it, the foreman. He's fine. Normal. No injuries at all. He's grinning. Behind him are a few other men I haven't seen before. They're wearing suits and look important. They're equally happy. One can't contain himself and is smiling way too hard.

The foreman rolls the TV over to the right side of my bed so I can see it without moving my neck. He tells me how excited he is to show me what they've been working on. He turns the TV on.

Security footage from the construction site plays. I see different angles of the site. Blue tinted interlaced video of workers doing their thing. No sound. The angle changes and I see myself. I watch the foreman and I walk through the site. I see him point the view out to me and I watch myself look out. The camera shakes with the building and I see my fear. I watch the foreman explain what we have to do. I lower myself into the hole and I fall. The angle changes and I can see the impact. I watch my legs break and my body crumple. If I wasn't watching footage of myself I'd think I just saw someone die. The foreman turns the TV off.

One of the other men grabs my shoulder gently and tells me what a great job I did. Everyone thanks me and is happy. They tell me this is going to be in a movie. A big movie coming out this summer and I did a great job.

I wake up.

Nightmare Meter: 5/5

Highway Crash

I'm driving on a highway in an old Ford cargo van. It's a pretty big highway, at least four lanes on each side. Every car around is me spinning out or they're driving in the wrong direction. It looks like we're all driving on an ice rink. Nobody can get their vehicle under control. There are cop cars blasting their sirens, but most are regular commuter cars, no massive trucks.

All the drivers and their passengers are screaming terribly. Everyone has their windows rolled down so every private whimper and cry for help can be heard. People begging for the carnage to stop. The only noise matching the screams are the crashes. Cars constantly collide with highway dividers or other cars. Bodies fly through windshields and become speed bumps for other drivers. The highway is littered with small fires and car carcasses.

I'm driving and doing my best to maneuver around the chaos.

I wake up.

Nightmare Meter: 3/5

Japan Poison

I'm in Japan for a few days with some friends. We meet up with two Japanese guys who show us around, one of which is Yuto Horigome, the pro skater. We walk around and have a laugh using my bad Japanese to interact with the locals. I only know how to say "ok" and "here" so everyone is cracking up while I try to buy things and talk to people with my shitty vocabulary.

We get in Yuto's friend's car and he drives us to another shopping district. Instead of music we listen to what sounds like a shortwave radio. It's slightly garbled and I can't quite make out what is being said, but I can hear the voice of a man. At first it sounds like talk radio, but as it goes on the repetitiveness makes it sound more like a distress signal. An SOS maybe. I don't have a problem with it though because I like the sound of shortwave radio.

We're walking around the new shopping district and I run into two friends I know from middle school. I haven't seen them for 10+ years. One has long dark shitty dreads like he's wearing one of those rasta halloween hats with the fake hair, but he's not wearing a hat so I guess they're real.

He's also holding a big bong with a horizontal chamber. Inside the horizontal chamber is a submarine sandwich. It feels like the weed equivalent of one of those bloody marys where they put a hamburger at the top. He's just walking around Japan with this sandwich bong like people walk around Vegas with those long yard drinks. I tell them I'm in Japan for three days and we should hang out while we're all here and they say, "Yeah," but I know

215

we're probably not gonna hang out.

Me, my friends, and our Japanese guides sit down at a restaurant. Someone orders champagne. When it arrives one of my friends looks at the bottle and says, "Nah, nah, this isn't the right one," and he sends it back.

The waiter comes back with a new bottle of champagne and my friend sends it back again. The waiter returns with a third bottle of champagne and tells us that we better like this one because he's not bringing back a fourth. This bottle is approved and we hold our glasses out for the waiter to pour us up.

The waiter tries to pour into my glass, but misses and hits the table. I don't want to waste it because it was such a hassle to get the right bottle so I move my glass under the edge of the table to try to catch the runoff.

I notice my glass is weird. It starts as a regular champagne flute but at the top it blooms outwards in all four directions like a flower petal. I also notice that nobody is speaking Japanese anymore. The waiters and the Japanese guys with us are all speaking English. We might as well be back in America. I catch the spilling champagne in my flower glass and give it a taste.

It doesn't taste right. I announce that this must be a bad bottle. I'm a little sad to make the waiter get a fourth, but something is wrong here. There's no carbonation at all. It doesn't taste *bad*, but it does distinctly taste off. Not like champagne.

I taste some more and my friends start looking at the bottle. Everyone is examining it and trying to find an expiration date or something. Nobody else wants to try it. There's a weird mark on the label. A slight panic sets in and everyone sharply agrees that nobody else should drink it. The bottle starts fermenting and bubbles rise out of the open neck. I should not have drank this. One of my friends rubs the label and it comes right off. It was a fake label. The bottle has been poisoned.

I stand up and feel someone lock their arm horizontally behind my arms and grab my collar. I think back to the shortwave distress signal I heard earlier. Help.

I wake up.

Nightmare Meter: 2.5/5

Home Invasion

I'm in a large house/compound with famous rapper/informant 6ix9ine. It feels like a compound that cartel guys would live in like in *Sicario* or real life. The environment is well populated with other guests, maids, cooks, security, and anyone else that would be at home in a compound. Everyone is actively saying shit like, "We have nothing to worry about. Nobody is going to try to kill 6ix9ine."

That sentiment is tested immediately when we all go to bed and Splinter Cell-type dudes infiltrate the compound and start fucking killing us.

I've got my belly on the floor and I'm crawling around this bedroom while a soldier looks through the window with his night vision scope. I can see his POV through his rifle's optics and there's an optical illusion hiding my body. Every time he scopes up I stop moving and because of the light I don't show up as a person on his night vision. He's too zoomed in and I just look like a part of the rug.

I'm sweating bullets trying to crawl out of the room and playing dead every time I hear the soldier shoulder his rifle. I'm almost out of the door, but he catches me moving and shoots me twice in the stomach with his silenced rifle.

I bleed out slowly on the floor. I don't know if they got 6ix9ine.

I wake up.

Nightmare Meter: 3.5/5

Godfather

The Godfather is not an American crime film directed by Francis Ford Coppola. *The Godfather* is a movie where one man was infected in an experiment gone wrong. Shortly after, his skin began to bubble and then he exploded. The people caught in the blast were not hurt, but they were covered in a thick black ash and became similarly infected. Soon their skin began to bubble and then they exploded and anyone caught in their blasts repeated the cycle. People infected in this wave are called "Godfathers."

Some become depressed and suicidal when faced with their impending doom while others wield their new power as weapons and infect other soldiers who want to willingly become Godfathers.

I can remember a scene where a terrorist took off a trench coat in a bank and revealed his pulsating skin. His skin bubbled like boiling water and everyone started freaking out because they knew he was a Godfather and about to blow. A woman covered her child with her body so he would not be infected in the blast.

I wake up.

Nightmare Meter: 1.5/5

Chips

I bought a second set of poker chips to match my first set, but these new chips are a slightly darker color so they don't match and instead of circles they're shaped like slices of bread.

I wake up.

Nightmare Meter: .5/5

Jaguar Jaw

I'm on a field trip to an animal rescue for school. Several picnic tables are spaced out where students sit and do worksheets. In the distance I see volunteers walk animals back and forth between their habitats. The volunteers are a mix of too young and too old, nobody in a true position of authority.

One of the younger volunteers is walking a massive black jaguar and a companion dog when he stops by my table and says he needs to station these animals here for a minute. He lashes the jaguar and dog to the end of the table. He reminds us that we should not pet or interact with the jaguar and then leaves.

Everyone else at the table seems content to ignore the animals and do their work, but I am fascinated with being so close to the jaguar. I don't break the touching rules set by the volunteer, but I examine the cat from every angle available to me without leaving my seat. Soon the jaguar notices me and begins examining me in a similar fashion.

I notice my classmates are getting ahead of me so I return to my worksheet. I try to bring my arm up to write, but I feel a tugging sensation. The jaguar has my entire forearm in his mouth. It feels childish or playful, not aggressive, but I still can't remove my arm. I'm not scared, but whatever excitement I had about being this close to the jaguar has vanished. I can't work on my worksheet either since I'm right-handed.

Nobody else at my table seems concerned that my arm is in the mouth of this huge cat. They all continue with their worksheets.

The jaguar rolls my forearm around in his mouth and I'm reminded of his incredible strength. I can feel the points of his teeth in my arm. Every few moments he exudes a modicum of extra force and I feel a twist of pain. It's so obvious how he could snap my arm in half if he wanted to. At the moment it doesn't seem like he wants to, but his grip is not loosening.

More rescue volunteers walk back and forth transporting animals. I try to signal their attention silently without alarming the jaguar any further. They ignore me just like my classmates, content to stay wrapped up in their work.

I start making more and more noise to attract the volunteers attention. They look up at me, see my entire arm stuck in the jaguar's mouth, and let me know they'll be with me as soon as they can. Nothing about their speech makes me feel like they're taking this seriously. They have the tone of indifferent employees, like they see this 1,000 times a day and it's somehow my fault they chained a huge cat to my table and it started eating me.

The jaguar doesn't seem as playful as he did before. Every time he adjusts his jaw I can feel my bones roll back and forth in my arm. These movements hurt seriously now. I can't see it, but I can feel that his teeth have pierced my flesh. The big bite that takes my whole arm off is getting closer and closer. I have to do something.

I yell at the parade of volunteers, "HEY YOU USELESS IDIOTS. THIS THING IS GONNA BITE MY ARM OFF!!!"

I slightly regret calling the volunteers useless when I see their reaction to my scream. They seem more concerned with being called useless than helping me, but at least I have their attention now.

One worker chains his animals to another fence and walks over to me. He makes a big show of how slow and out of the way this movement is. He ambles my way and stands over me. He sighs and lowers his eyes at me as if to say, "What do you want me to do about this?"

He unhooks the jaguar and dog from my table and tells me he's gonna lead them in the opposite direction. He tells me I will need to pull my arm backwards when he starts walking.

I steady my self and grab my trapped right arm with my left. Nothing about this seems by the book, but this is the best option I guess. He's the expert.

I'm about to start pulling my arm out of the jaguar's mouth, but it's no longer in his mouth. The jaguar has spun around and now I'm elbow deep in his asshole. It's gripped tight around my bicep like a blood pressure monitor.

The jaguar starts to walk away, but as he does his asshole prolapses and turns inside out. My arm isn't moving out as much as the jaguar is moving away, but his asshole continues to grip my arm and slowly slide down it. The animal keeps walking and the prolapsed asshole eventually slides down to my hand and releases me.

The volunteer doesn't say a word about any of this, just keeps walking like I wasted five minutes of his valuable time.

My arm is covered in ass slime. It's so sticky. I don't think I can return to my worksheet without getting butt juice all over it.

I wake up.

Nightmare Meter: 3.5/5

Concert

I'm going to a concert for a rapper I know. He usually performs in small venues, but this is a huge step up. The line wraps around the outside of the building and down an incline that wraps around even further. The venue itself is an old schoolhouse. At least four or five stories. The windows are crooked or falling off, chimneys jut out at improper angles, the whole building might fall over if a strong enough wind blows through.

I walk down the line looking for the end and notice there are signs placed at different intervals that allow you to cut depending on the color of your wristband. I look down at my wristband and it's white. I walk past signs for blue, red, purple, and every color except white. The white wristband seems to be the shittiest level and I have to get in line at the absolute back.

While waiting in line I realize I have a backpack on. Nobody else in line has a backpack and I begin to worry I won't be able to get in with it on. I'll need to find a stash spot so I can pick it up after the concert. I have a water bottle in my backpack I really don't want to lose.

Even though I'm close to a half mile away from the entrance, the line is beginning to move much faster. I turn around to see how far I've come and see a beautiful girl behind me. She looks like a grown up version of a girl named Lily I knew in middle school. I ask if she's Lily and she replies, "Yes, but not the one you knew in middle school." How does she know about the Lily I knew in middle school if she's not her?

I approach the front door of the venue and step inside.

225

There's a crack under the stairs I stuff my water bottle in. With that gone I bunch up the rest of my backpack and cram it into my back pocket. I walk further into the building and see no signs of security. Beginning to feel like I didn't need to get rid of my shit.

I can hear muffled sounds of the concert, but I want to take a piss before I get fully involved. I start walking up these old creaky steps looking for a bathroom. I walk up and up without seeing any signs of anything, let alone a bathroom. Eventually I see my first door with an arrow sign that says "RESTROOM."

I get closer to the door and am heartbroken to see that it's a women's bathroom. While I'm looking at the sign the door swings open and I briefly see Lily inside washing her hands. She sees me see her. I'm worried she thinks I followed her.

I return to the stairs and keep walking up. After climbing to the top of the building I finally find a second door. It leads me to a classroom that doesn't seem to have been used in years. The desks are misaligned and covered with dust. I see a wall-mounted crank pencil sharpener. I don't think modern classrooms have those anymore so this has got to be old.

I walk into the classroom to see if there's a bathroom connected at the back. No luck. There doesn't seem to be anything else in here so I turn to leave and am confronted by a small goblin in Jedi robes.

He can't be more than 4 foot tall and his face is glowing dark green. I can't really tell if this is some sort of demon or just a small person dressed up for the concert. I walk towards the door and the demon strafes with me. Despite his small stature he makes it clear that he's blocking the exit. He locks eyes with me and I feel an intense fear wash over my body. There is no misunderstanding here. He wants to hurt me. Not before I hurt him. I prepare to wind up a huge soccer kick to deliver into this freak's head.

I wake up.

Nightmare Meter: 2/5

Drone

A drone crashes outside my house in the country. I'm living in a farmland area with a huge swath of open space and no neighbors. I follow the smoke to a giant bale of hay where I find the crashed drone.

I inspect the wreckage and realize that I've seen this before. This drone was on the news recently. It shot down a helicopter that had a prominent political activist inside.

The drone is not sized like a real UAV, it's more like a large camera drone. Maybe five feet in length. It doesn't make sense how something so small shot down a helicopter, but I know that it did. I saw it on the news. I open a hatch on the drone and scroll through the touch screen menu.

Upon reading the menus I discover that this is a government drone and they orchestrated the activist's murder.

The drone wakes up. Its broken rotors twitch like it's trying to take off. Lights switch on and flash a distress beacon. Someone knows where the drone is.

I turn it off, wipe it down for prints, and run back to my house. I'm terrified that another drone will show up soon to kill me.

I wake up.

Nightmare Meter: 2.5/5

Restaurant Casino

I'm on a work trip to Atlanta. The crew is staying downtown in some apartment buildings. It's been a long day and everyone is excited to go somewhere fun for dinner. It's decided that we should go the crown jewel of downtown Atlanta, a combination restaurant-casino called *Hittler's*. There are two t's so it's ok that it's named that.

The dinner crew has a broad mix of ages. I'm the youngest by far, most of my co-workers are 10-20 years older than me, and then a chunk of senior citizens came too. Not sure how they got the invite, they weren't working with us. I think they were just excited at the idea of anyone going to Hittler's and had to tag along.

Hittler's is located in a sprawling outdoor mall. It feels like one of those Chinese cities that's 20 stories above ground level. I look down and see dense spiraling staircases that lead to designer stores, clubs, and more apartments.

The old folks in our group are leading the charge. We're allotted no time to be tourists. The idea of eating at Hittler's has them moving like they're forty years younger. They're zeroed in, completely unfazed by the mall's many distractions. I'm lagging behind because I'm trying to find one of those mall signs with an arrow pointing to Hittler's. I think it would be funny if I got my picture taken at the Hittler's sign or at least got a picture of the sign without me in it.

I'm unable to find a suitable sign and I'm starting to get left behind so I cut my losses and catch up with the group. Maybe I can get a picture on our way out. We take an elevator down and arrive at our destination.

Given the futuristic nature of the rest of the mall, I'm a little disappointed at how tacky Hittler's is. It looks like a Denny's with gold foil accents. It's a diner with mostly booth and bar seating.

A small hallway spills into the "casino" that features a spattering of slot machines, an unmanned craps table, and one sad blackjack table. Most of the tables have ashtrays on them so I guess you can smoke here. All of the old folks we traveled with file into the casino and find seats at the slot machines.

The rest of us sit in a booth and take a look at the smallest menu I've ever seen. It's a laminated note card. About as big as your hand. On that note card are seven meals. No drinks, no sides, no substitutions. You tell the waitress the number you want and that's what you get. I read the note card over and over hoping something will grab me, but nothing looks good. I excuse myself to use the restroom. Maybe after a quick piss I'll come to a conclusion for dinner.

The bathroom is a long walk away. So long that in the scheme of the mall I'm not sure if I'm still in Hittler's. When I left the table I didn't really have to use the bathroom, but by the time I get there I truly need to piss. I walk in and my heart breaks when I see a line in front of me.

Three guys crowd the entrance to the bathroom. Beyond those three guys are two bathroom attendants. The bathroom itself is barely big enough to hold two stalls, we're way past max capacity with me in here. I'm about to exit to wait outside when one of the attendants calls to me. He tells me to come in, there's an open facility. I guess the other guys are waiting to shit. I slide past them further into the bathroom.

There are no toilets in the bathroom. There are no urinals either. What is here is a recumbent exercise bike that's been modified with a bedpan. The seatback leans all the way down so you're practically lying horizontal when you're using it. There are no other toilet options, if you want to piss/shit you have to pull your pants down and sit in the bike.

The bike isn't even facing the wall. It's facing the entrance where all the other guys are waiting. Nobody wants to use the bike toilet so they're letting me jump the line. I circle the bike slowly, trying to see if there's something I'm missing here, but I understand the contraption all too well. The bathroom attendants nod at me. One wipes the seat down with a towel, encouraging me to give it a spin.

I'm good. I don't think I'll use the bathroom at Hittler's.

I wake up.

Nightmare Meter: 2/5

Internet Guy

I'm in my room. It's not actually a room I've ever lived in, but in this dream I know it's my room. I'm sitting in a beanbag chair using my laptop with blankets up to my neck. I'm cozy. A guy comes in.

I've never seen this guy in real life, but it's a guy I think is funny online. He's known for pushing boundaries. I didn't invite him in or know he was coming. I'm not even scared that somehow he got into my house, but he's here and he wants to hang out.

There's a little bit of an awkward vibe because I'm under all these blankets and have my laptop up. He doesn't say anything, but I can tell he's worried that he's walked in on me jacking off. I shake the blankets off and stand up. His uneasiness vanishes as he sees I'm a normal guy and I'm not jacking off. I was just being cozy and using the computer.

We hang out and have a fun time together. He shows me a new video he's been working on. For some reason he shows me the video over Zoom even though we're in the same house. We're on a Zoom call with a third screen playing the video and I invite another one of my friends to the call to watch the video too.

The video is called "X has a bad day" or something like that. I can't really remember specific details of the video, but it had the Internet Guy abusing his friends and doing dumber and dumber shit. It ended with him saying the n-word in public and getting arrested.

I think the video is really funny, but my other friend doesn't think it's as funny as I think it is. The Internet Guy ends up bullying my friend a little bit when he tries to give honest feedback and I feel bad for inviting my real friend to this. It feels cool I'm getting a preview of his work though.

The call ends and I'm back in my room. The Internet Guy is standing there at the doorway, but the mood has changed drastically. We've been having fun all day, but now it doesn't feel like that at all. I don't exactly want to leave, but I'm a little uncomfortable that he's blocking the exit. I realize for the first time how big he is. At least 6'4" and not fat, but big. Strong.

The Internet Guy steps aside and reveals another big man behind him. This guy is wearing a gimp mask and I see a flicker of light. The gimp is holding a long broom pole and pointing it towards me. There's something attached to the end of the pole, but because of the head-on angle and a glare I can't make out what it is.

He moves closer to me and moves the pole out of the light so I can see what I'm facing. There's a knife taped to the end of the broom pole.

An evil smile develops on the Internet Guy's face. The same smile he had when he was bullying my other friend. I look at the pole and think that the knife isn't that long (maybe 3 inches max) so I should be able to grab the pole before the knife gets to me if he attacks.

The gimp approaches me and slowly lunges. It's an incredibly telegraphed attack, but I'm still too slow to react. I grab the pole as the knife pierces my chest. Too late.

I wake up.

Nightmare Meter: 3.5/5

Baby Cabin

I'm in a log cabin and there is a wall full of baby legs. Besides the baby leg wall everything is normal. There's a couch, side table, lamp, fireplace, rug, etc. About what you would expect from a classic log cabin setup. The details are not as memorable because the defining piece here is the baby leg wall.

This wall is covered in severed baby legs mounted like hunting trophies. Sometimes when you see a mounted deer head they're stuck to a little wooden shield thing, but these legs are straight glued to the wall. There's no interference in the leg to wall contact.

Most of the legs have intact knee joints. They stick out knee up and form a 90° angle as the rest of the leg hangs vertical. Most of the legs are like that. A chunk of other legs are mounted upside down or sideways so the knee is locked and the whole leg just sticks straight out.

But maybe 25% have broken knees. These legs are bruised and stick out at angry inhuman angles frozen by rigor mortis. There's maybe 200 legs on the wall. The broken ones look like they were easy to break. Like snapping a crab leg.

I wake up.

Nightmare Meter: 4/5

Delivery

I'm paying $70.64 for two sandwiches off Postmates and that's before tip.

I wake up.

Nightmare Meter: 1/5

Club Night

It's club night and I'm out with my friends. We have a larger than normal group. Like when you go out with friends and those friends invite their friends and all of a sudden there's like 14 people in your group. It's a good feeling to be out with so many people. A fun night is ahead of us.

The club is in a large warehouse downtown. The space is so big and so sparsely lit I can't see any of the walls. I can't even see the ceiling. Total darkness in all directions.

Spread throughout the darkness are couches with groups of people dancing around them. There's a lot of people, but the space is even larger so it's easy to move around. It's lacking the normal shoulder to shoulder congestion of a club. Most people are wearing all white.

The piano intro of *Dreams and Nightmares* by Meek Mill starts to play and everyone turns up a notch. The Philly national anthem. Our group is going crazy. I put my right foot up on a couch and with the assistance of a friend, launch into a huge backflip.

By the time I land the party is ending. House lights come on and security guards shake their flashlights to signal that we need to leave. People were getting too rowdy and they had to shut it down. Hillary Clinton was going to come out next too, but due to the behavior of the audience she is staying backstage. People seem genuinely bummed that we missed Hillary. It feels like I'm the only person who doesn't care that we are missing Hillary.

I'm walking out with my friends when I realize I have no shoes on. They must have been thrown off when I did the backflip. My wallet and keys are gone too. Everything flew out of my pockets except for my phone. I start backtracking to try and at least find my shoes.

Out of the darkness a pair of shoes with their laces tied together is thrown at me. I think someone is trying to return my shoes at first, but when I pick them up I see they're not mine. I keep walking and see huge piles of clothes on the ground. People are rifling through the piles, taking some pieces and throwing others aside. A few scavengers are grabbing single shoes and running away with them. Some of the shoes might be valuable.

These thrift piles go on for miles in the dark, each one illuminated by a spotlight. If I can't find my shoes at least I can grab some replacements out of a pile. I dig into one and grab some mismatched DC/Osiris-looking skate shoes. They're too big for my feet so I lace them as tight as possible. I wish I had laced my original pair that tight, then they wouldn't have flown off when I did the backflip.

I backtrack to the exit to catch up with my friends. Outside of the warehouse there's a grassy area with small hills. It's good backflip terrain. I think about doing another one, but decide against it.

I keep walking and debate sending an embarrassing "Where are you guys I got left behind" text to the group. Thankfully I come across a bar/restaurant and see two of my friends smoking outside.

I go into the bar and sit down at a table with my friends. I'm relieved to see all my missing things are spread out on the table. Shoes, keys, wallet, and even some things I didn't think I had lost like my Leatherman. I thank my friends for retrieving my stuff and ask where they found it. Some security guard returned it as they were leaving. It surprises me that the guys who returned my stuff are probably the guys in the group that I am the least close with.

An older veteran waitress comes up to our table and tells us that they're kicking everyone out. Everyone that was using has got to go. She apologizes and lets us know she thinks our group is fine, but it's too late and they have to close because of other reckless parties. A heavily tattooed man is being escorted out when he pulls a knife on the waitress.

He holds the knife to her throat and presses her back to the wall. Even in the fear soaked room the waitress shows no emotion on her face. She's seen this 1,000 times before. She announces to the concerned crowd, "He's not gonna wanna do that."

My first thought is to run, especially if this psycho is the first of many to be kicked out. I'm about to take off when I hear the switch of my Leatherman's knife unfolding. I turn and see one of my friends has taken my tool off the table and armed himself. It seems like my friends are preparing to fight rather than flee. A little selfish of them to use my weapon in the melee without asking me, but I wanted to run so it's understandable.

I turn back around to see the waitress. The wrong-do-er has pushed his knife into her throat all the way up to the hilt. He drags the knife deep across her neck and opens her up like a pez dispenser. He removes the knife and her body drops.

I wake up.

Nightmare Meter: 4/5

Mulholland Drive

I'm sitting on a couch with two of my friends. One of them is sick. I put on *Mulholland Drive* and we start watching. I've never seen *Mulholland Drive* before so Kyle McLaughlin and Laura Dern are both in it.

McLaughlin keeps putting his hands on walls and flashing back and forth through time. The wall dissolves and he flashes into Dern's arms where they embrace and make out. It's a very confusing film and I can tell my friends are enjoying it much less than me and I'm barely enjoying it. One scene shows a static shot of a dimly lit doorway. It's one of the more exciting moments.

I reflect on the fact that I put this movie on without asking my friends if they want to watch it first. I feel especially bad for my friend who is sick. He should be watching something much lighter. I feel guilty.

I wake up.

Nightmare Meter: 1/5

Beard

I'm rolling around in bed half-awake, I haven't committed to getting up yet. I can feel that it's early and it's a weekend so I'm trying to go back to sleep. My eyes are still closed.

I'm not breathing totally right. That's what stopping me from getting back to sleep. I give a quick inhale through my nose and discover it's blocked. With my eyes still closed I throw a finger up there and start picking. I can feel a sticky booger and know if I can just pull that thing out I'll be cleared to go back to sleep.

I give the boog a good pull, but it doesn't budge. It's in there tight. I let go and reform my grip. I've really got it between my thumb and forefinger now. I pull a second time and rip it out. It feels amazing. I can breathe again.

I open my eyes just a crack so I can throw this thing in the garbage and I get a good look at it. Attached to the booger is a massive clump of hair. It's maybe 6-7 inches long and thick enough to use as a paintbrush.

I'm fully awake now. I get out of bed and go to the bathroom. I look in the mirror and my entire beard is gone. Everywhere where facial hair once grew is now covered with bloody open pores. I wipe my face and bloody my hand. Droplets fall from my chin and stain the white sink red. The pores covering my face look like what happens when a hair transplant is rejected. Somehow I pulled the wrong booger and ripped out all my facial hair through my nose.

I wake up.

Nightmare Meter: 4/5

Toilet Race

I'm standing in a circle with a group of people. We are in a great hall in an ever greater building. It's so great it might be a castle. In the middle of the circle is our teacher giving us instructions on our next task. We are to be dismissed individually from the group in 10 minute intervals and then run to the top floor where we will find a room with a toilet. We're then supposed to piss in the toilet and run back down to the area we started in. This will test our parkour skills.

Two or three people down from me in the circle is my girlfriend. As our teacher is wrapping up the instructions I move out of the circle and pull my girlfriend in close to kiss her. As my lips leave hers I feel sickeningly embarrassed. Why did I do that. Why did I kiss my girlfriend in the middle of class. Very much a move that a guy who has never had a girlfriend would do. I don't show my embarrassment on my face and thankfully neither does she. The test is about to start and I pray that one else clocked the weird thing I just did.

I'm up first. The teacher blows the whistle and I take off. I'm flying through the castle to a huge spiraling rectangular staircase. The empty space in the middle might measure 50 feet across. The staircase is enveloped by matte black scaffolding. They aren't much help running up the stairs, but I make a note that when going back down I'll be able to do some crazy parkour moves with them to improve my speed.

I reach the top of the stairs and see a door. I open that up and I'm in the bathroom with the toilet. I'm about to start peeing, but I notice a second door on the opposite side of the room. The only way into the bathroom is the door I came in, this second door leads to a dead end room. I hatch a plan to lock the door I came in through and then move the toilet to the second room and piss it in there. This might buy me some extra time in case one of my classmates is close behind me even with the 10 minute buffer.

I grab the toilet and easily move it to the second room. I place it on the floor and piss into it. I flush it. I pick it up to move it back to the first room when I realize my grave mistake.

I just flushed a toilet that was not connected to anything.

The water/piss initially went down, but is now re-gurgling back up into the bowl. The piss is coagulating and forming disgusting scrambled egg looking combinations. Behind the piss some nuggets of shit from the last person to use the toilet are starting to surface too. The water level continues to rise.

As I walk the toilet back to the first room the motion causes waves to rock in the porcelain. The toilet is much heavier now. Disgusting coagulated piss and shit is rocking back and forth. It keeps rising and rising until some of it starts to launch out of the toilet and onto the ground. I'm gonna throw up, but I have to get the toilet down first.

I place the toilet down where it originally was and see a disgusting trail of shitpisswater behind me. All around the toilet seat and floor are concentrated globs of piss and shit nuggets. I briefly consider cleaning it up (I hate when people leave messes in public places), but I'm ill equipped.

There's only toilet paper and it's so thin that if I touch any of this gross shit it will be like touching it with no toilet paper at all. I resign to leaving the bathroom in its current state. Maybe I'll have so much space between me and the next student that they won't realize I was responsible for this mess.

I unlock the door to leave and two people are standing right there waiting to go in. I won't be getting away from this. Fuck it. I rush down the stairs and start effortlessly swinging through the scaffolding like an ape. Even though my parkour is perfect I feel sick inside. Why did I move the toilet. That didn't save me any time at all.

I wake up.

Nightmare Meter: 2.5/5

School Shooting

A school shooting is happening in a classroom near me. When it first starts I hear the screams and I immediately escape into the hallway to make a run for it. I run as fast as I can away from the sounds of gunfire. I'm turning corners and I keep looking back to ensure no one is coming for me. I run and I run and I reach a dead end.

I catch my breath and realize I'll have to double back and look for another exit. While sucking air I take a second to listen for more shots. I don't hear any.

It's raining.

I listen to the pitter patter of rain drops on the tin roof. A big drop hits the roof and it echoes through the hall. This sound continues and I realize I can't hear the gun shots or screams anymore, just the rain. Another big drop hits and it's even louder than the last. I start to question what I heard. Did I really hear shots and screams? Or was it just the rain and a loud kid?

I ease back down the hallway and peer into a classroom. A teacher watches over students as they work in groups. Middle school aged kids, maybe 5th-7th grade. They look unbothered. I open the door and walk inside.

The teacher has a buzzed head. I can't remember if she pulled it off or not. I don't want to cause a panic so I casually walk over to her and tell her that I think a school shooting is going on.

While I'm talking to her I hear another knock on the door. A police officer steps in and tells us the lockdown is over. We can leave now.

Myself, the teacher, and most of the kids leave the

classroom and start walking back down the hall. We return to the original classroom I started in.

The wall with the chalkboard is riddled with bullet holes. There are no bodies, but there is blood everywhere. We walk closer and I can see that blood is seeping out from each bullet hole. The wall is bleeding.

Everybody starts to take pictures on their phones.

I wake up.

Nightmare Meter: 4/5

2021 PRESS JUNKET - WILL SMITH

INTERVIEWER: It's been twenty years since *Ali* released and you were first nominated for Best Actor. How has your mindset changed from then to now going into this year's award season?

WILL SMITH: It would be nice to win obviously, but the butterflies that used to plague my stomach are long gone.

INT: Did that take 20 years?

SMITH: It might have. I was recognized at the Grammys much earlier. You'd think that would kill any nervousness, but the Academy Awards is a totally different environment. I felt like I belonged at the Grammys. I knew I had done something worthwhile when I was nominated. I love *Bad Boys* and *Independence Day* as much as anyone else, but it took some time to build that same confidence with acting.

INT: I never would have guessed, you always seem so comfortable in your roles.

SMITH: Thank you, but that's mostly apathy you're seeing.

INT: Apathy? You don't care?

SMITH: Yeah, once I started making this much money, I

completely stopped caring. Who gives a shit, right? *Bad Boys 4? Men in Black 3?* Fuck it ok.

INT: You don't care about your roles? Then why do them?

SMITH: Do you know how much money I made from *Men in Black 3*? I made eight figures off the backend. $100 million. From one movie. Took me less than a year, I could've done another movie and made even more if I wanted to. It's gross. $40 million for the tennis movie. I'm doing a slave one too and they're giving me another 35. It's so gross. I look at my bank account and I'm sick to my stomach. But not sick enough that I'll ever stop. Hard to feel anything at an awards show when you have half a bil. Hard to feel anything anywhere.

INT: You don't feel?

SMITH: I feel. I feel like a god that's for sure. So what if they give me a statue. Give it to somebody who needs it because god—I—know I don't.

INT: Where do you find meaning then, if not in your work?

SMITH: That's interesting. Let me show you. How much money do you make?

INT: I don't see how that's relevant.

SMITH: Of course you don't, it doesn't matter. I think we

both know whatever you make is less than $400,000, is that fair?

INT: Sure.

SMITH: I'll give you $400,000 right now if you can eat an apple to its core in under 25 seconds and you don't question whether this is a sexually interesting activity for me to observe.

INT: You're joking.

SMITH: Here's an apple. [Smith pulls an apple out of his jacket] Go for it. The only rule is before you start you have to tell me you're trying. You have to look me in the eyes and tell me you're going to try to eat the apple for money. Then you can start and if you succeed, the money is yours.

INT: I don't have to put up any money? I can just try and eat it without risking anything?

SMITH: Money? No, but you're risking everything by trying it. You are risking your complacency. Your life is going to split after this. This will become the defining moment of your existence. Imagine you eat the apple in 24 seconds. How often will you face hardship and think how much easier things would be if you had been one second faster. Your car will break down and you will think how close you were to a windfall. Your basement will flood and you will daydream about the different class of life you barely

249

missed. You will hold your mother's hand and tell her goodbye while you think how close your were to effectively treating her cancer.

INT: Start the timer.

SMITH: You're forgetting something.

INT: I'm going to try to eat this whole apple in 25 seconds for $400,000.

SMITH: Yeah, that's right. You are, aren't you. Five, four... three... two.......one. Start.

[The interviewer begins eating the apple and Will Smith walks out of the room]

10 Places to Visit Before You Die

1. My best friend's sister's pussy.

2. My best friend Roger's sister's pussy.

3. I had sex with my best friend Roger's sister's pussy and it felt sooo good it felt amazing.

4. I've been best friends with Roger since we met in third grade and we've shared every piece of our lives with each other, but now that I'm having sex with his sister there is a piece I can not share.

5. I look into my best friend Roger's eyes and know a carnal intimacy that he could never and should never imagine.

6. My best friend Roger's sister is a total freak and I think she's that way because of something that happened to her which makes me uncomfortable, but not uncomfortable enough to ever bring it up ever.

7. I go to the movies with my best friend Roger and he offers me popcorn without knowing that last night I stuck my cock in his sister's mouth and told her to breathe through her nose like a good girl.

8. I know it kills my best friend Roger because it would kill me too so every day I thank god nobody can fuck my sister because she died when she was seven months old from SIDS.

9. Paris, France

10. I will kill myself, Roger, and his sister if anything stops what is now happening to my dick from continuing to happen.

2006 PRESS JUNKET - FOREST WHITAKER

INTERVIEWER: Forest—

FOREST WHITAKER: You seem like a tough guy.

INT: Oh. Ok, thanks.

WHITAKER: Big strong guy. Think you're a big strong guy huh?

INT: No, not really.

WHITAKER: Do you deadlift? What do you bench? How about we take our dicks out and see who's bigger, huh? Sound good, playboy?

INT: No?

WHITAKER: [Whitaker pulls himself out of his zipper] Here's what I'm working with. Right here. Now let's see who's bigger.

INT: What.

WHITAKER: Oh, I can see you through your pants. I can see it all.... and yours is bigger? By a wide margin? Probably because you saw my dick and got hard. So you weren't really playing fair now were you?

Comics

I'm not very good at drawing so please imagine these comic ideas in your own mind.

COMIC #1

A genie is summoned from a lamp and he says, "For freeing me you have earned three wishes!" and then underneath that he has a thought bubble that says "PleaseDon'tFuckMe, PleaseDon'tFuckMe, PleaseDon'tFuckMe."

The guy who freed the genie is saying, "Oh wow, three wishes. I'll have to think about this..." and his thought bubble is blacked out and says "FUCKTHEGENIE" like 100 times.

COMIC #2

A hitman is handed a large envelope of cash and told to "Make it look like an accident." The next panel shows him in a crowded area violently shooting a guy in the head and saying, "Whoopsy-daisy."

COMIC #3

A man is jacking off in a drive-thru while the employee asks him, "Sir, is the meal gon be a medium or a large?" He's thinking about how someone once told him to always jack off before you make an important decision.

COMIC #4

A Chinese restaurant has a "C" health inspection grade in the window, but next to it they have placed duplicate letter signs that spell out "HINESE FOOD."

Thank you for your participation in imagining these comics.

2016 PRESS JUNKET - RYAN REYNOLDS

RYAN REYNOLDS: You remember the last time I sat in front of you? What I told you? Was it three? Three years ago for *R.I.P.D.?*

INTERVIEWER: I wasn't gonna bring it up. Honestly, I wasn't sure if you'd remember talking about it.

REYNOLDS: Are you kidding me? I've been trying to get this made since 2009. It's more of a surprise that I'd sit in front of anyone and not talk about it.

INT: I have to give you credit, the movie is not only amazing, but it came out exactly the way you described it three years ago.

REYNOLDS: I had the vision! You have to have a vision to get something like this made. Pitching it felt like I was trying to tell studios that I could see the future and most of them reacted that way too. I just couldn't see a reality where this movie was not a hit. Shame it took six years for anyone else to see it too, but hey, we got there.

INT: The work shows. Any other examples of future-telling you can share? I'd love to get in on the ground floor of the next *Deadpool*.

REYNOLDS: If I had something I'd love to share it. For now I'm taking a breather and enjoying the film just like all the other fans.

INT: During prod—

REYNOLDS: Actually wait. I do have some future-telling I can share. It's definitely not what you had in mind though.

INT: Oh, please. I'm all ears.

REYNOLDS: Ok. This is something I've noticed recently. But. Oh my god, I can't believe I'm saying this. Ok. I can smell. I can smell my shit before it comes out.

INT: What do you mean by that?

REYNOLDS: My shit. Like my poo.

INT: Oh, you mean "shit" literally.

REYNOLDS: Yeah.

INT: I'm still a bit confused.

REYNOLDS: So I can smell my own shit before it happens. Like I sit down on the toilet. I haven't shit yet, but I can tell I'm going to because I can smell it. Before it comes out.

INT: You can tell you're going to shit before it happens.

REYNOLDS: Yeah. Because of the smell.

INT: Ok.

REYNOLDS: You get it now?

INT: Kind of.

REYNOLDS: I guess I can tell the future in more ways than one, huh?

INT: Yeah.

REYNOLDS: It seems like you're still a bit confused.

INT: No. I understand what you're saying.

REYNOLDS: What am I saying?

INT: You're saying you can tell the future because you smell your poops before they happen. You sit down on the toilet and smell poop and that's how you can tell you're going to poop.

REYNOLDS: Pretty neat right.

INT: Yeah, um yeah. Definitely.

REYNOLDS: Speak your mind. I can tell you have more questions about this phenomenon.

INT: No, really I get it. I don't need to hear anything else.

REYNOLDS: Come on man, we're friends here. Shoot.

INT: Ok. Well. You say you sit down on the toilet right? And you smell shit?

REYNOLDS: Yes. But before anything comes out. Like it's a smell premonition. I can smell the smell of shit. Then like two minutes later I open up and shit.

INT: Ok. That's what I thought.

REYNOLDS: Cool, right?

INT: Yeah. I just think you're smelling shit that's already there.

REYNOLDS: What do you mean? I haven't shit yet. That's the whole point, I'm smelling it before it comes.

INT: I get the idea, but I think what is actually happening is you sit down on the toilet and then you smell shit that's already on your ass. Like you're not wiping enough. You sit down and smell your last shit, not the one coming.

REYNOLDS: What the fuck are you saying to me? I don't wipe enough?

INT: That's what it sounds like to me. If you sit down on the toilet and smell the shit on your ass.

REYNOLDS: That shit's not funny, I don't need to hear some hack shit joke shit from you.

INT: It's not a joke, I'm not joking. I get it, it happens sometimes. You don't always...get it all you know? But if you're consistently sitting down on the toilet and smelling shit. Yeah...you are probably not wiping enough. You are smelling your own dirty butt.

REYNOLDS: I'm 40 fucking years old I know how to wipe my own ass.

INT: It doesn't sound like it.

REYNOLDS: Is this a put-on? Did Blake put you up to this? To fuck with me like this?

INT: To fuck with you? You brought this up. You said some insane shit like you can smell your own shit before it happens. Why did you say that?

REYNOLDS: BECAUSE I CAN! That's why I said it!

INT: You're not wiping your ass right man. Maybe try a bidet or something.

REYNOLDS: A bidet? Yeah right, what do I look like, a faggot? Oh my god. The instant I said that I wanted to take it back. Are you rolling right now? Are both the cameras rolling?

INT: ....

REYNOLDS: You need to delete that. Seriously. Both the camera guys and the audio guy. Need to delete all of that. That needs to be gone right now. You know I don't hate gay people—I actually like some of them—but you were taunting me. It felt like you were gunning for me from the jump. The instant I started talking about the smelling thing you were gunning for me. You wanted your 15 minutes with a snappy "gotcha" on an A-lister when I was fucking opening up to you. I was being vulnerable and you took advantage. You were trying to hurt me and I reacted—which was wrong—but we are both to blame for this. Both camera guys need to delete that now.

INT: Relax, they can delete it.

REYNOLDS: Delete it. You heard him.

CAMERA OPERATOR: It's all one take so it's kind of hard to delete it and Ava is AC/DIT so she should be the only one pulling media.

INT: Ok, they might not be able to delete it right now, but our AC can include a note to post with the timecode to scrub that when they get the cards.

REYNOLDS: Include a note to post, yeah I'm sure. Why are you saying shit like that like I don't know what an AC is? Where's Ava?

CAMERA OPERATOR: She's 10-1.

CAMERA OPERATOR 2: 10-2 probably.

INT: You know I think we can wrap this up. We got enough for the junket, so don't worry about staying and I promise you we'll delete it. You're good.

REYNOLDS: "Delete it," I'm sure. I could hear the cash machine ringing off in your head when you heard me say fag. *Cha-Ching. Cha-Ching. Cha-Ching.* This is why you're you and you—none of you—will ever be me. You could live your life a million times and a million times you'd still be sitting in that chair and never in mine.

INT: Thanks for your time Ryan, we appreciate it.

REYNOLDS: Ok. Ok... ok listen. What if. What if I let you record me saying, "gook." A recording of me saying fag gets out and I'm done. My career is finished, I can't come back from fag. But *gook*... I'll be ok if I say gook. Gook will hurt me sure, but it won't ruin me like fag would. How's that for a deal, huh? A fair trade. We all leave happy if I say *gook*. We have a deal? Ok, hit record now I'm about to say it.

MORE SCRAPS

INT. ITALIAN RESTAURANT - NIGHT

Tommy is eating a big plate of spaghetti and doing the worst Godfather impression possible.

> TOMMY "TWO LICKS" DISCARPA
> I hear you've got a nice business opportunity working for you.

> BILL
> I do, Tommy, I do. And I mean no disrespect. I came to you as soon as I saw the money start to come in.

> VINCENT "GREASE TRAP" MAIONE
> That was the right move, eh? Nobody wipes their ass in this city without Two Licks's blessing.

> TOMMY "TWO LICKS" DISCARPA
> Nobody.

                    BILL
Hahaha, you know I wouldn't do
anything like that, right?

        VINCENT "GREASE TRAP" MAIONE
You wouldn't wipe your ass? Get a
load of this guy! He wouldn't wipe
his ass!

        TOMMY "TWO LICKS" DISCARPA
Ha ha ha hee haa ha ha ha hee hu hu
ha hee ha. HUm.

                    BILL
Haha. So, how do I make this right?
I don't want to step on nobody's
toes or nothin.

        TOMMY "TWO LICKS" DISCARPA
You want to do business in this
town, it's real simple. You gotta
suck off Jimmy "Da 8-Year-Old."

                    BILL
What?

        TOMMY "TWO LICKS" DISCARPA
You want to keep running game? Fine
by me. As long as you suck off Jimmy
"Da 8-Year-Old."

                    BILL
I'm sorry, I heard you. Who's Jimmy?

                    VINCENT "GREASE TRAP" MAIONE
Jimmy "Da 8-Year-Old" is who you
gotta suck off if you want to keep
that street business of yours up
and running.

                            BILL
Yeah. Ok. I don't know if I can do
that.

                    TOMMY "TWO LICKS" DISCARPA
This is the game. And you're in it.

                            BILL
This is the game?

                    VINCENT "GREASE TRAP" MAIONE
Jimmy's in the back. And he don't
like to be kept waiting.

                            BILL
There's gotta be something else I
can do, right? 30%, 35% of my take
is yours!

                    VINCENT "GREASE TRAP" MAIONE
It's not about the take.

                    TOMMY "TWO LICKS" DISCARPA
This is not up for negotiation.
This is how it works. You wanna do
business in my city? You suck Jimmy
off.

                            BILL
Jimmy the eight year old.

                            265

                    VINCENT "GREASE TRAP" MAIONE
Jimmy's in the back.

                              BILL
I can't do this. I'm not even gay.

              TOMMY "TWO LICKS" DISCARPA
Being gay don't got nothin to do
with it. It's about respect.

                    VINCENT "GREASE TRAP" MAIONE
This guy's gay.

                              BILL
You can't be serious.

Grease Trap takes out his gun.

                    VINCENT "GREASE TRAP" MAIONE
Do we not look serious?

                              BILL
He's not. He's not actually.
     (whispers)
It's just a name right?

              TOMMY "TWO LICKS" DISCARPA
What he say Grease Trap?

                              BILL
It's just a name right? Jimmy? He's
not
     (whispers)
actually eight?

                    VINCENT "GREASE TRAP" MAIONE
Jimmy don't got all day.

                    BILL
I don't think I can do this guys.
I want to do business I really
do. I never seen this much money
in my life. But if this is what it
takes...

          TOMMY "TWO LICKS" DISCARPA
You think you're the only two-bit
wannabe gangsta who had to suck off
Jimmy "Da 8-Year-Old?" You're far
from the first and you won't be the
last.

                    BILL
Other people have done this?

          TOMMY "TWO LICKS" DISCARPA
Ol Rollo, Jake "Sock Puppet" Persica,
Frank "The Pedophile" Terranovo.

                    BILL
I'd guess Frank didn't have much of
a problem with it did he.

          VINCENT "GREASE TRAP" MAIONE
If they're doing business in our
city? They sucked him off.

                    BILL
So he's not. Eight then. He's an
adult, right? That's what I thought,
but the name kinda threw me.

          TOMMY "TWO LICKS" DISCARPA
Mansfour.

                    BILL
He's four?!?

        VINCENT "GREASE TRAP" MAIONE
It's a metaphor. His name.

                    BILL
Jimmy is older than four right?

        TOMMY "TWO LICKS" DISCARPA
Much older.

                    BILL
How much older?? More than four
years older than four right? Much
older than that???

        VINCENT "GREASE TRAP" MAIONE
Jimmy's old enough.

                    BILL
Ok. Ok I'll do it. But if I go back
there and it's a kid—

DING! The door opens.

        FRANK "THE PEDOPHILE" TERRANOVO
Fratelli!

        TOMMY "TWO LICKS" DISCARPA
Frank!

        FRANK "THE PEDOPHILE" TERRANOVO
Two Licks, good to see you. I've
come to pay my respects. I've opened
a new business.

                    VINCENT "GREASE TRAP" MAIONE
That's the fifth new business you've
opened this week!

                         BILL
I should not be here.

INT. OFFICE - NIGHT

> EMPLOYEE 1
>
> You heading out?

> EMPLOYEE 2
>
> Yeah.
>
> (THIS NEXT LINE SHOULD BE
> DELIVERED SARCASTICALLY.
> IT SHOULD BE CLEAR THAT HE
> DOES NOT WANT TO RUSH HOME
> FOR MEATLOAF NIGHT. EVEN
> THOUGH HE IS HEADING HOME
> HE IS NOT EXCITED ABOUT
> EATING MEATLOAF MADE BY HIS
> WIFE. AGAIN, I DON'T MEAN TO
> HAMMER THIS POINT HOME, BUT
> IT NEEDS TO BE CLEAR THAT
> HE IS NOT GENUINELY EXCITED
> FOR MEATLOAF NIGHT. THIS
> IS SARCASM AND HE ACTUALLY
> IS NOT LOOKING FORWARD TO
> MEATLOAF NIGHT)
>
> Gotta rush home for meatloaf night.
> What about you?

> EMPLOYEE 1
>
> Ahh, I'm probably gonna stay a
> little longer. Burn some of that
> midnight oil.

> EMPLOYEE 2
>
> You work too hard, man. You need to
> give yourself a night off.

EMPLOYEE 1

Hey, I can feel a promotion coming
and if a couple extra hours seals
the deal, I'm putting the time in.

EMPLOYEE 2

You definitely deserve it. What's
this been, every day this week you've
stayed late? I know I couldn't do
it.

EMPLOYEE 1

It's only a few hours. Nothing
crazy, but I'm hoping it adds up.

EMPLOYEE 2

I'm sure it will. Don't work too
hard, I'll catch you tomorrow.

EMPLOYEE 1

Yep, see you tomorrow and—hey. You
know I'm just working here, right?
Just working normally. Finishing up
some spreadsheets, compiling the
data, stuff like that.

EMPLOYEE 2

Yeah. Have a good night, man.

EMPLOYEE 1

I just want it to be clear that I'm
doing normal work, but for longer.
When I stay late at work I'm doing
that to do more work. Not to do
anything else here alone.

EMPLOYEE 2
I know, man. You want that promotion.
I get it. I'll see you—

EMPLOYEE 1
I've got the spreadsheet right here.
Got it up on my monitor—my big one.
That's what I'm working on right
now. Quarterly numbers. You can see
it right here. If I wasn't working
on it, it wouldn't be there, right?

EMPLOYEE 2
I've gotta go. Just get some rest
at some point.

EMPLOYEE 1
        (loudly)
I know **you've** gotta go. You do that
and **I'll** stay here. At the **office**.
To do **more work**.
        (whispers)
Listen, I've got this big promotion
coming up, you know it I know it
everybody in the office knows it.
All I need is a little more time
and the promotion is mine. What I
don't need is everyone believing
some made-up unsubstantiated rumor
that I'm staying late every night
to *jack off* in the **office** instead of
doing work, ok?
        (loudly)
NOW DRIVE SAFE!

                    EMPLOYEE 2
What? Nobody thinks that? Are you
doing that?

                    EMPLOYEE 1
NO! I'M **NOT** DOING THAT!
        (whispers)
I'm staying late in the office to
work because I think if I put in
some **extra hours** the bosses will
see that and reward me. And if you
think that's a lie then check my
trash can!

                    EMPLOYEE 2
I'll see you tomorrow.

                    EMPLOYEE 1
It's just normal stuff in here!
        (puts hand in trash can and
        combs through it)
Junk mail, food wrapping, chip bag,
no cum that I can see!

                    EMPLOYEE 2
...

                    EMPLOYEE 1
Go ahead! Look for yourself.

Employee 1 dumps the trash can out.

                    EMPLOYEE 1
What's in the trash can?

                    EMPLOYEE 2
It's trash-trash was in the trash
can. Now it's on the floor.

                    EMPLOYEE 1
If I was really jacking off in
the office wouldn't there be some
evidence in here? I mean, chip bag,
food wrapping, don't think so! They
lock the bathrooms at night so if
I was staying here to jack off then
where's all the cum?

                    EMPLOYEE 2
I don't care what you do here at
night as long as you are not doing
it near my desk. If you are actually
trying to get a promotion though,
definitely do not tell anyone else
that you're jacking off in the office—

                    EMPLOYEE 1
ARE YOU LISTENING TO ME? THAT'S THE
ONE THING THAT I'M NOT DOING. I'M
WORKING LATE. LOOK AT MY FUCKING
MONITOR. IT'S A SPREADSHEET.
MICROSOFT EXCEL. QUARTERLY FIGURES.
          (he starts locking the bottom
          drawer on his desk)
I GOT A PROMOTION COMING UP. DON'T
LOOK IN THIS DRAWER. THERE'S NO CUM
IN THERE. JUST MORE SPREADSHEETS.
HOW WOULD I EVEN GET THE CUM IN
THERE UNLESS I BENT MY SHIT DOWN
AND AIMED IT INTO A HOMEMADE DRAWER
CUM CATCHER.

Employee 2 is already gone. Employee 1 wipes
the sweat off his brow.

                    EMPLOYEE 1
Whewwwww. Close one.

He starts unbuckling his pants and unlocking the drawer.

                    JANITOR
        80% of the time you try to shoot
        loads into that drawer you miss and
        I gotta mop it up.

INT. FOYER - NIGHT

SHONDA

I watch the news now. I never used to do that. I used to stay up and read or write poetry. And now every night I watch the evening news. Every night. Do you know why? Do you care?? It's because it's the only way I'll ever know what you're doing. You leave Friday and I won't see you until Tuesday. I'm glued to the screen waiting until I hear about a shooting or a raid or a car chase and pray I don't see your shoes getting pushed into an ambulance. You're not a kid anymore! You run around with these thugs like you're still 17!! You have a kid your damn self!! Don't you want to see him grow up?! You say you do what you do for us. For your family. But if you really loved us you would leave the streets behind. We should move to Africa.

JEFF DUNHAM

I'm not leaving the streets. That kid isn't mine and even if he was he's boring as hell. I'm not leaving the streets. You're crazy if you think I'm leaving the streets. If you think I'm going to Africa you're a moron and you need to get a job.

SHONDA

Do you like seeing me cry? What
kind of husband comes home and
makes their WIFE CRY?

JEFF DUNHAM

You're drunk, you're wasted, you
need to go to rehab, you think you
can have brunch every day of the
week. You're nuts if you think I'm
moving to Africa.

INT. PERFUME OFFICE - DAY

                    PERFUME SALESMAN
This scent is a song. Opening
stanzas bring forth hints of rose
and bergamot which twist into a
melody of milk and soft oriental
notes.

                    PERFUME CEO
I've traveled all over the world
and smelled over 1,000 scents don't
talk to me like I'm one of the kids
you fuck.

INT. LIVING ROOM - NIGHT

                    DIANE
Oh my god, this guacamole is so
good.

                    PEDRO
          (mouth full)
Shho gooud.

                    DIANE
You swear you made this? You didn't
send Jacob to Little Oaxaca before
we came?

                    MIRANDA
Swear to god. Made it right in the
new kitchen.

                    JACOB
I can vouch, I even chopped the
onions.

                    MIRANDA
He made one cut before I had to
confiscate the knife.

                    JACOB
Hey! You didn't need to tell them
that.

                    MIRANDA
Hahaha. I know how that goes. I
trust Pedro with Pop-Tarts and
that's about it.

                    PEDRO
I've got Pop-Tarts down though.

The dog Cooper comes in. He starts pawing at the table.

                    JACOB
Oh, oh, oh! Look who wants to join
us!

                    DIANE
I can't get over how cute he is!

                    MIRANDA
He's like, "Uhh Mom, you forgot a
plate for me!"

                    DIANA
Hahahahaha.

                    JACOB
Do you want some people food, Coop?

                    COOPER
Bark! Bark!

                    MIRANDA
He's like, "Yeah! How many times do
I have to say it?"

The door bell rings.

                    MIRANDA
Oh, that's Emma. I'll be right back.
Actually, Jacob, can you follow me
with the trash?

                    JACOB
Right behind you, babe. Be back in
a sec. Don't let the place burn
down!

                    DIANE
Not a chance with this guy here!

Miranda and Jacob leave. Diane pets Cooper.

                    PEDRO
So that was fucking crazy right.

                    DIANE
The guac's good sure, but like we
definitely had better in Mexico
City.

                    PEDRO
No, not the guac. How did Miranda
know what he was thinking?

                    DIANE
Who?

                    PEDRO
Cooper. The dog. Cooper barked and
Diane could almost... understand
him. She... I don't know... Has some
kind of connection with Cooper...

                    DIANE
What are you saying?

                    PEDRO
I've never seen anything like that
before.

                    DIANE
It's a dog. He has maybe like three
different thoughts.

PEDRO
Yeah, but... how did she know?

DIANE
You're joking, right? Miranda isn't
Dr. Doolittle. She's just messing
around, doing the dog mom thing
everybody does. Talking for him.

PEDRO
Yeah, ok. Sure.

Miranda, Jacob, and Emma come back.

MIRANDA
Look who I found!

EMMA
Oh my god, Diane!

DIANE
Emma!! It's been so long!

PEDRO
Hey, Emma.

JACOB
Margaritas anyone?

EMMA
Please tell me it hasn't been since
Charlotte's wedding.

DIANE
I think it has. I can't believe it,
it's so good to see you!

                    MIRANDA
Sit! Sit! You're on drinks, Jacob?

                    JACOB
On it, babe.

                    MIRANDA
Please help yourself, we made way
too much food.

                    DIANE
Don't sleep on the guac.

                    EMMA
You don't have to tell me twice.
Oh. My. God. Is this Cooper?

                    MIRANDA
You haven't met him?

                    JACOB
He was staying with my Mom when we
first moved in because of the paint.

                    EMMA
Miranda, this dog is gorgeous. I've
seen pictures on IG, but in real
life he's like a model!

                    COOPER
Bark!

                    MIRANDA
He's like, "Thank you! Model is
kind of what I'm going for."

                    EMMA
Hahahaha.

                    JACOB
Margs almost done, everyone wants
one?

                    DIANE
Yes, please!

Jacob walks over with four margaritas.

                   MIRANDA
Emma, please tell us everything
about work. I can't believe you're
doing the new Pixel campaign!

                    EMMA
It's been seriously crazy. We were
pitching for weeks before we got the
contract. You know what actually?
One of our ideas was supposed to
feature a dog and it was getting
a good response. We ended up going
another direction, but Cooper would
have been perfect for it.

                   MIRANDA
Please don't tell me that because
I'm dying for the day his Instagram
takes off and I can be a professional
dog mom.

                    JACOB
Hear that, Coop? Maybe next time.

                   COOPER
Bark! Bark!

PEDRO

He's like, "I want to get fucked by
Pedro."

MIRANDA

What.

DIANE

Pedro?

PEDRO

Right? That's insane. I can't
believe he said that. I wonder why
he said it though...

MIRANDA

What did you say, Pedro? Is that a
joke or something?

DIANE

He's-he's joking.

PEDRO

Hey! If anyone's joking it's him!

Pedro points to Cooper.

DIANE

Woooooooowwwwww.

JACOB

Let's take a breather here.

MIRANDA

You know Cooper's like our kid,
right? That's not funny. It's not
funny to joke about having sex with
our dog.

                    PEDRO
I was just doing what you were
doing! I didn't say anything! Your
dog is craaazzzzyyyy though.

Pedro slides closer to Cooper.

                    JACOB
Hey, don't come any closer to Coop.

                    MIRANDA
I don't know about where you're
from, but we don't fuck dogs here.

                    PEDRO
Woah! First of all, your dog wants
to get fucked by me, you fucking
moron. Were you even listening to
him? I didn't say shit. I don't
want to do anything.

                    DIANE
Hey, Pedro isn't from anywhere. He
grew up in North Hills.

                    MIRANDA
I don't care where he grew up, don't
joke about fucking my dog!

. . .

                    EMMA
Any more... margaritas?

                    JACOB
I think we're out.

                    PEDRO
Hey. Listen. I'm sorry about this.
Big mix up. I don't even know what
happened. Let's just go back and
try to have a good time.

                    JACOB
You know, we've got a really big
day tomorrow. I think we might just
wrap it up.

                    COOPER
Bark!

                    PEDRO
He's   like,   "PedroIWantYouToFuck
MeHardAndShootHumanCumInMy
Stomach."

                    MIRANDA
What the fuck!

                    JACOB
You need to leave.

                    DIANE
Don't worry, he is.

                    PEDRO
Your dog is crazy, we should get him
out of here before he says another
crazy thing. I'll take him to the
basement.

                    MIRANDA
GET THE FUCK OUT OF MY HOUSE!

                         PEDRO
Hey! No need to freak out. Lose
control. We're leaving.

                         DIANE
I'm not going home with you.

                         PEDRO
Oh, you too? Real mature, Diane.
Their dog says a couple crazy things
and I'm the bad guy. For listening.
Just because I'm from North Hills.

                        MIRANDA
You are saying this bullshit! The
dog can't talk!

                         PEDRO
Oh, now the dog can't talk? You
seemed to understand him pretty
well earlier?

                         JACOB
Dude, you seriously need to get the
hell out of here. I'm gonna call
the cops.

                         PEDRO
I'm leaving. I'm leaving. I can
read a room. I don't even have my
DB anyway so I can't do anything.

                         EMMA
What's a DB?

                         PEDRO
DB? A dog barrel?? You can buy them
online. Like a barrel with four

straps on it. It comes in 3 different sizes depending on how big the dog is. The site says it's for aging liquor but everyone on K9LoveForums uses it for something else.

                    JACOB
Yes, police, I have a man in my house who won't leave.

                    PEDRO
You guys all know Jacob has only dated black girls, right? Whole life, only black girls. Since he was like 13. If you stopped being black Miranda he would break up with you.

                    DIANE
What is wrong with you?

                    JACOB
We need an officer now.

                    EMMA
How would she stop being black?

                    MIRANDA
GET THE FUCK OUT! GET THE FUCK OUT!

                    COOPER
Bark!

. . .

                    MIRANDA
He's like... "Pedro...you need to leave."

                    PEDRO
Oh, wow. Ok. I didn't know you
wanted me gone too. Hey. I get it.
I hear you loud and clear, boy. I.
Am. Outtahere. Leaving pronto.

Pedro turns around to walk to the door.

                    COOPER
Bark!!

Pedro immediately unzips his fly and pivots.
He launches himself at Cooper, but crashes
mostly into the coffee table and fucks
everything up. A huge piece of glass is
wedged into his throat. He chokes on blood
and spits it up into the guac.

INT. DINING ROOM - NIGHT

                    WIFE
So even though I had proof that I
sent the original confirmation email
Gil still took Rachel's side and
blamed me for the miscommunication.

                    HUSBAND
I'm sorry.

                    WIFE
It's-it's unbelievable. Even if she
didn't get the email—which she did—
she still has the time and location
on her calendar. I know she gets
calendar alerts so she ignored two
separate notifications telling her
when and where the meeting was.
It's not my fault that she doesn't
check her calendar!

                    HUSBAND
Yeah, absolutely.

                    WIFE
Absolutely... yeah. What am I
talking about again?

                    HUSBAND
Sorry, what?

                    WIFE
The last ten minutes or so? What am
I talking about?

HUSBAND

Oh. Come on. Work and fucking Gil, what is this?

WIFE

What is this? Just my life! I don't know. I thought my husband would be interested in it for some reason.

HUSBAND

Baby... I am. I'm sorry. I-I've just been... I hate to keep saying this, but I'm still adjusting. I'm not used to this yet. I want to. So badly do I want to. But...

WIFE

No, it's ok. I know—I mean I don't know, but... I'm just so happy you're back. I love that you're here, but sometimes you're sitting right across from me and it feels like I'm still waiting for you to come home.

HUSBAND

Baby. I'm here. I promise I'm here. I love you.

WIFE

I love you too.
    (beat)
You know you can talk about it with me. If you want to... if you think that would help.

                    HUSBAND
I know. I know I can. I think it
might help. When I'm ready.

The Wife smiles at her Husband. She starts
doing the dishes.

                    HUSBAND
We used to split them in half.

                     WIFE
Huh?

                    HUSBAND
The   Afghans.   The   people   in
Afghanistan. We used to split them
in half.

                     WIFE
What do you mean, baby?

                    HUSBAND
There's train tracks in Afghanistan,
not a lot, but there are some. And
we'd take Afghan people and put
them on the train tracks. Then when
the train comes it would split them
in half.

                     WIFE
I don't understand.

                    HUSBAND
We'd split them in half longways.
You tie them to the tracks, but just
one track, not like in the movies.
Then peg their arms and legs into
the ground so they're splayed like

hands and feet both out. Then when
the train comes it splits them in
half.

                WIFE
Oh.

                HUSBAND
Shhhhhp. Pow. Right down the middle.
Balls to skull.

                WIFE
Why. Did you do that?

                HUSBAND
Just following orders I guess.

                WIFE
You had orders to split Afghans in
half?

                HUSBAND
No. No I guess nobody told us to do
that. We just started doing it.

                WIFE
So. Why did you do it?

                HUSBAND
You've never split anyone in half?

                WIFE
No.

                HUSBAND
Yeah, it's not as common in civilian
life. You wouldn't get it.

                    WIFE
Did you do this a lot?

                  HUSBAND
I don't know.

                    WIFE
How many times did you do it?

                  HUSBAND
They'd never brake which is strange
because the trains were always
driven by Afghans so they were
always running over their own guys.
Probably saw us and were afraid
stopping the train would cause more
problems then just soaking it and
splitting a couple of their own
guys in half.

                    WIFE
A couple?

                  HUSBAND
Yeah. Sometimes we'd tie a few down.
The trains don't come so often so
you'd want to tie a few down per
train. Else if you had more guys
you wanted to split, you might have
to wait til tomorrow for the next
train to split them.

                    WIFE
I don't know what to say.

                    HUSBAND
    Talking about it helps. You were
    right. I'm feeling better.

The Husband starts aggressively chowing
down. He's forking the food so hard that he
hits clean through to the plate and makes a
terrible screeching noise.

It sounds like train tracks.

INT. BEDROOM - NIGHT

                    MARK
That's so crazy. I don't know what
to say.

                    SOFIA
You don't have to say anything.

                    MARK
Thank you for opening up. I
appreciate you trusting me with
something so personal. I know that
took courage. I see how much courage
you have for carrying that for so
long. You're so brave.

                    SOFIA
Thank you. I want to believe that,
but sometimes I don't feel very
brave at all.

                    MARK
Your little brother huh. That's so
crazy.

                    SOFIA
Yeah.

                    MARK
Cuz usually it's the older one. Like
you were probably much bigger than
him. It's crazy you got molested by
your little brother. Cuz I remember
you saying he didn't know what
dial-up was so it wasn't like he
was just a year younger than you.
He was probably like four or five

years younger than you. And girls
go through puberty faster than
boys. So if you were 15, what was
he? Like eleven?. Ten? I don't even
know how he pulled that off. Hats
off to him I guess. I don't support
it at all, but it's so crazy. Like
insane.

                    SOFIA
Yeah.

INT. DINING ROOM - NIGHT

> FRANCO
> Cheers! To new friends and old.

Franco takes a big drink from his mug.

> FRANCO
> So. Misty. Hhhow. Hhooow haas uyourr hah-aarrt been. Beeeen coohhmminngg. Aallllonng.

> MISTY
> Franco? Are you feeling ok?

Franco's vision is blurring. The room is spinning. He can't find his balance. He can't focus on anything.

> FRANCO
> Ohhhh. Iiii. I ddoonnn't knnnooww.

Franco's head falls to the table. His eyes glaze over, but he manages to lock his gaze briefly on his mug.

He grabs for the mug and pushes it off the table.

It shatters.

> FRANCO
> Thee.... Thee cuum... Someeoonee pooissoneed thee cuuumm....

> MISTY
> You're the only one who drank cum.

                    DENNIS
You came in here, took out a bottle
of cum, poured it in that mug and
drank it.

                    MISTY
Fast. You drank it very fast.

                    FRANCO
Sommmeeebody. Gottt to thee cuumm.
Andd tampeerrred wiith iiitt.

                    DENNIS
You said he's done this before?

                    MISTY
It's crazy how fast he drank that
cum. Like he chugged it and it was
a full mug. I don't even know where
he got it all from.

INT. OFFICE - DAY

              GUY AT WATER COOLER 1
Yo.

              GUY AT WATER COOLER 2
Yo.

Guy 2 fills his paper cup at the water cooler.

              GUY 1
So, you know how I've been seeing
that new girl?

              GUY 2
New girl?

              GUY 1
Oh yeah. New girl. Big fuck up. I
fucked up bad. Colossal fuck up.

              GUY 2
Can't be that bad.

              GUY 1
We've been seeing each other almost
every night. She's already got a
toothbrush. Practically lives at
my place. So almost every night
we're... you know. It seems great,
right?

              GUY 2
It does.

              GUY 1
Right? And it's good too. She's
really pushing it forward, which

is great, but last night man. Last
night she's poking and prodding me
before bed. I can tell she's about
to ask me if I would be okay with
something. I'm no bitch you know,
but the way she's dancing around
this shit has got me a little
nervous. She's talking about how
much respect she has for me and how
much trust she has in me and she
knows that I respect her too and
all this. It's practically a speech
she's giving me. It feels like she
practiced this and probably given
it to other guys before.

                    GUY 2
Uh oh.

                    GUY 1
Yeah. So finally I'm just like, ok
what's going on? And then she asks
me. Just lays it out. She asks me
if I would be okay with calling her
the n-word when we fuck.

                    GUY 2
No fuckin way.

                    GUY 1
RIGHT? Fucking nuts. My jaw is
pretty much on the floor and she's
telling me she knows it may be
uncomfortable for me as a white
guy, but it would be a huge turn on
for her. She literally wants me to
do this.

                    GUY 2
She wants you to—

                    GUY 1
And fuck me, right? What are my
options? Of course I say no, but
she's not having it. She's telling
me more shit about trust and all
this shit about how she wouldn't
ask if she didn't really "believe
in us." And I'll be honest, I didn't
want to stop the train when it was
starting to pick up speed. You know
the way things were going I was
ready for her to pull out a strap-on
or tell me she wanted another guy
to come over. So definitely crazy,
but I was ready for way worse.

                    GUY 2
So you—

                    GUY 1
Yeah, I'm an idiot. I fucking said,
"ok." This is where I fucked up.
I didn't ask for more details. I
didn't ask for context. I should've
gotten direct instructions on how
and when and where, but I didn't.
I thought I could figure it out for
myself. I set off on this great road
trip without a fucking map.

                    GUY 2
You're driving without a map?

                    GUY 1
I might as well be drunk driving a

peterbilt.
        (beat)
We get into it. Things are going
fine, normal...and she starts...
sucking my dick.

Guy 2 nods.

                    GUY 1
I'm looking down and I'm trying to
enjoy this. I want to enjoy it,
but all I can think about is, "Ok.
Should I say it now?" I'm looking
for the right moment, and to be
honest, I really wanted to step up
for her. All that trust talk got to
me. I didn't want to let her down
or make her think I'm weak or I
can't hang or something. So yeah—

                    GUY 2
No.

                    GUY 1
I'm not gonna tell you what I said—

                    GUY 2
I can imagine what you said. I am
imagining what you said.

                    GUY 1
As far as things go with what I
said. I'll say this... It could
have been worse. It could have been
much, much, worse. I definitely said
what I said, but from a completely
objective third party stance—

                    GUY 2
Which you're not.

                    GUY 1
I took it pretty easy on her.

Guy 2 stops filling up his cup at the water
cooler. It's been overflowing this whole
time.

                    GUY 2
So how long until—

                    GUY 1
Immediately. Immediate stoppage. I
watched in real time as she realized
how much she does not like the thing
she asked for and how stupid I was
for giving it to her.

                    GUY 2
She wasn't happy?

                    GUY 1
No. She was not happy.

                    GUY 2
What did she say?

                    GUY 1
She annihilated me, man. I barely
managed to not get kicked out of my
own apartment.

                    GUY 2
No like, literally. What was she
saying. What did she actually say.

                    GUY 1
I was too fast. I said it too soon.
I couldn't wait to say it.

                    GUY 2
Could you?

                    GUY 1
...

                    GUY 2
How long before you said it.

                    GUY 1
I have no fucking clue man.

                    GUY 2
More than 30 minutes?

                    GUY 1
Does it matter?

                    GUY 2
More than 15 minutes?

                    GUY 1
I don't know.

                    GUY 2
Really. More than five minutes?

                    GUY 1
Yeah, ok. It was probably more than
five.

                    GUY 2
How long was it.

GUY 1

It was. Like, maybe seven or eight I guess.

GUY 2

I bet it was like four.

GUY 1

I wasn't looking at a fucking clock man. I don't know.

GUY 2

Sounds like three or four. You said it too fast.

GUY 1

IT DOESN'T FUCKING MATTER. I could have given her four fucking hours of foreplay before dropping that bomb and it would not have been enough. There was no right time or moment or method. I was set up to fail. You know *WarGames*? "The only winning move is not to play."

GUY 2

Yeah I don't watch movies, but I know what you mean man. Been there. Married for sixteen years and I'm pretty sure my wife is poisoning me so whenever she cooks I feed a piece to the dog first. It was working for a few years, but the dog died a few days ago because I guess you're not supposed to feed them grapes and she made me a meal with grapes in it.

                         GUY 1
          I'm done dating white girls.

INT. HIGH SCHOOL CLASSROOM - DAY

                    MINDY
          (sobbing)
Oh my god. Oh my fucking god. I
don't want to die!

                  CHRISTINA
The shots are getting closer!

                    MAX
We should all hide in the closet.
That's the safest place.

                   MINDY
He's gonna kill us!! He's coming!!

                  OLIVER
We should barricade the door. Let's
push all the desks in front of the
door so he can't get in.

                  MARCUS
We have to be ready. If he does get
in somehow... we have to rush him.

                  PAVLOV
What if we start ringing a bell and
giving him food? Then the next time
we ring the bell he will be really
hungry even if we don't give him
food.

INT. PORN SET - DAY

> PRODUCER
>
> Ok. Camera's up? Sound? Let's just roll through all this. Great. Lexi, how are you feeling? Good? Is that your real name? Should I call you Lexi?

> LEXI
>
> No, but yeah. You can call me Lexi.

> PRODUCER
>
> Amazing. Can we kick these lights up a bit? Ok, Lexi. You've signed the model release form, but we just want to snag some wild lines before things get sticky, yeah?

> LEXI
>
> Yeah, sure.

> PRODUCER
>
> We want to maximize our discoverability so let's run through some keywords and then our editors can remix this for different markets. Can you say, "I'm a barely legal teen?"

> LEXI
>
> I'm a barely legal teen.

> PRODUCER
>
> Great, so good. Now, "I'm a Latina hooker."

                    LEXI
Umm. I'm a Latina hooker.

                  PRODUCER
Keep em coming. "I'm a big booty
black hooker. I'm a slutty Chinese
hooker.   I'm   an   Indian—wait.
Indigenous hooker."

                    LEXI
I'm white.

                  PRODUCER
Yeah. Well, yeah obviously. We're
gonna color correct this. Switch
your whole color around. Play with
your eyes. You can do a lot in post.
I think we're shooting in S-Log?

              CAMERA OPERATOR
S-Log3.

                  PRODUCER
S-Log3, so we've got a lot of
flexibility in regard to what race
you appear as on camera.
     (beat)
We'll come back to that. So you
signed the release which is great.
You're over 18?

                    LEXI
I'm 18 and a half.

                  PRODUCER
Awesome, that's so cool. Wow.
Obviously this is all above board
and we would never actually film with

                     311

someone below 18, but artistically, right, there is a good deal of room for implications.

                    LEXI
What do you mean?

                  PRODUCER
Cinema is all about imagination, right? Well we want to play with the audience's imagination. Can you fire off a couple lines like, "I don't remember 9/11. I've never seen a phone that's not an iPhone. Oh, I have so much 8th grade math homework to do later."

                    LEXI
I have so much 8th grade math homework to do later.

                  PRODUCER
Great, really great. That's gonna crush in Japan.

               CAMERA OPERATOR
I need to swap batteries quick.

                  PRODUCER
Go for it. I was talking to your agent earlier and he said you have a special kind of signature move you do?

                    LEXI
Yeah I do.

                    PRODUCER
What is that?

                      LEXI
I do this move where I fuck the
shit out of him.

                    PRODUCER
Wow. That's amazing. We'll have to
save that for the end. Make sure we
get proper coverage for when Lexi
fucks the shit out of him.

                      LEXI
Can we start?

                    PRODUCER
For sure. Almost. I've just got
this quick list of activities we
need to get through and then we can
get started. I'm gonna run through
this list and you just tell me if
you're comfortable doing that on
camera or not, sound good?

                      LEXI
Yep.

                    PRODUCER
And due to some stricter workplace
regulations that have been getting
enforced lately, I can't exactly
say what I'm asking you, if you
understand that. We've kind of got
to... dance around it a bit. But
you're bright I'm sure you'll pick
up quick. So, do you consent to
having fun with Damien over there?

                              LEXI
I do.

                            PRODUCER
Great. And would you be ok if Damien
had fun on your face?

                              LEXI
Yes.

                            PRODUCER
If maybe you were having fun with
your mouth would you be prepared to
swallow some fun on camera?

                              LEXI
For sure.

                            PRODUCER
Great, great. What if Damien got
tired of having fun with you, but
he didn't want the fun to stop so
he called in three or six of his
friends. Would you have fun with
his friends too?

                              LEXI
I've got no problems with *having
fun*. I'm a pretty fun girl.

                            PRODUCER
I bet, I bet. This is gonna be
some pretty rough fun though. Don't
get me wrong, it'll be fun, but
also these guys will really be
having the majority of the fun. The
lion's share of the fun some might
say. You'll still be having fun,

but compared to the amount of fun these guys are gonna be having, I think most viewers would agree what you're doing doesn't look very fun at all.

                    LEXI
Ummm. Ok.

                  PRODUCER
There might be some fourth wall breaking. Like maybe you start begging me to stop the fun, but the guys just hold you down and keep having fun with you. Like the fun doesn't stop even if you want it to!

                    LEXI
...

                  PRODUCER
Obviously if you actually want to stop having fun, we'd stop the fun right there. But for the camera I mean. It might be interesting if you were just begging for the fun to stop, like crying, and throwing up and spewing bile and cum and snot all over their cocks—

               CAMERA OPERATOR
Yo.

                  PRODUCER
Shit, sorry. My bad. I mean. Once we get going we don't want the fun to stop! All in good fun, right?

Hahaha. Ok. We have the Angenieux on? Great. Ready, Lexi?

                    LEXI
I'm not sure.

                    PRODUCER
Well, we've got a whole stable of fellas back there who've been railing cocktails of speed and sildenafil. They've been watching Family Guy Lois Hot Compilations for a few hours so they're ready to go. We're gonna send em out two by two until you're fucked into a small unrecognizable paste.

                CAMERA OPERATOR
Still speeding.

                    PRODUCER
Sounds like fun, right? Any last questions?

                    LEXI
They're all clean, right?

                    PRODUCER
Clean? Of course Lexi. You know what? Probably they are. Let's get into it, huh? We're gonna do a couple of takes here, but for this first one? Just try and have fun with it.

INT. MANOR - DAY

                    DENVER
     I think that covers it for intros.
     The floor is now open to any questions
     or comments. Anything you want
     to talk about, please feel free.
     That's what this group is for.

                    AMY
     Hi. Well. I'm having an issue with
     one of my guys. Maybe not an issue
     actually. He's amazing, an amazing
     guy. The perfect worker—the issue
     is he's performing so well and I'm
     struggling to find a way to reward
     his hard work.

                    DENVER
     Ahhh, ok, we've seen this before.
     Anyone have any ideas on how to
     show appreciation to one of your
     guys?

                    PAUL
     I know when one of my guys is going
     above and beyond I like to send
     some extra food his way at the end
     of the day.

                    DENVER
     Extra food, great. Shows you're in
     tune with his needs. Anything else?

                    SUGGS
     Some new shoes? Manual labor can
     be hard on the body and the right
     equipment can make it much easier.

                         317

                    DENVER
Shoes, food. How are these options
ringing for you Amy?

                     AMY
Well. I have spoken with him and
he's actually been pretty forward
with what he wants.

                    DENVER
Oh, fantastic. Well, what's the
issue then?

                     AMY
It seems he's quite set on freedom
actually. He'd like to be freed.

                    DENVER
Ahhhh. Well. Well obviously we're
not just going to free one of our
guys.

                     AMY
No. No, I didn't think so.

                    DENVER
Ok. Other ideas. What can we do for
our guys besides free them?

                     PAUL
Maybe. A day off?

                    SUGGS
Come the fuck on, Paul, we're not
giving our guys a day off.

                     AMY
He might like that.

PAUL

It was just an idea, man.

SUGGS

Well, it kind of defeats the purpose of having guys, right? The whole point is we don't give them days off. They work all the time.

DENVER

Suggs is right, obviously we're not giving our guys a day off.

PAUL

Does anyone else feel a bit funny about this whole situation?

AMY

Maybe? Like, I guess we get days off, but our slaves don't.

SUGGS

Woah, woah, easy there. We uhh, try not to use that word.

DENVER

There's a bit of a connotation to it.

AMY

Connotation to what?

DENVER

To, uhh...slavery.

AMY

Oh.

                    SUGGS
Ok, I've got something. What if you
get him a hat.

                     AMY
He's got a hat already. I don't
think a slav—guy... should have two
hats.

                    SUGGS
Wait. A hat that says "Number 1."
Lets him know that he's the best
worker, show off a bit to his friends.
Might boost his self-esteem?

                     AMY
Ok. Could do. First thing that
comes to mind is I don't think my
husband will love it. He kind of
sees himself as the "Number 1?" He
might react poorly if he sees one
of the guys thinking they're above
him.

                   DENVER
Maybe some smaller text that
clarifies he's the number one guy
and not number one overall.

                    SUGGS
Maybe a hat with his name on it?
What's your guy's name?

                     AMY
I don't know I think we took his
name away from him.

                    PAUL
Yeeeuughhh. Ughh. Ok. This. All of
this. Does anyone else feel weird
about it?

                    SUGGS
They can have a hat, Paul. Relax.

                    PAUL
Ever since we started these meetings
I've been feeling less and less right
with this situation. I thought the
talking would help. Maybe it did a
bit at first. But lately it's been
doing the opposite.

                    DENVER
What are you saying, Paul?

                    PAUL
Should we be... having guys at all?

                    SUGGS
Jesus, Paul.

                    PAUL
I look at my life and I have so
much. I look at theirs and something
in my stomach feels sick. That's
it. And if I can do something to
change that, change that feeling,
shouldn't I?

                    AMY
You're fucking insane. This guy's
insane. We should kill you.

                     321

                    DENVER

Nobody's killing anyone. But Paul.
This is our way of life. Who are we
to play god and change it?

                     PAUL

I'm not saying get rid of them. But
what if we treated them like we
treat each other? For starters we
could pay them.

                    SUGGS

This guy is insane and we should
kill him.

                    DENVER

For the good of the group I have to
end this line of conversation. Paul,
we are praying for you and hope you
can come to the next meeting with
clearer heart and mind. However, if
you bring this tomfoolery up again
we may be forced to bar you from
this social club and possibly kill
you. OK! Any other issues we can
discuss?

                     AMY

I've got another problem with my
girls were my husband won't stop
fucking them? What can I do about
that?

                    SUGGS

There is nothing you can do about
that.

CUT

I like to get fucked up. I like to get so fucked up I can't see or breathe. I like to make people worried. I like to lean on walls and out of chairs and drool on myself because I've been chewing the same piece of gum for 20 minutes and my saliva is pooling up. I like to spit on the ground. I like to climb trees and fall out of them. I like to walk four miles home because my phone died when I got to the bar and I like the way it feels when someone sees me walking and how cool they must think I look for walking four miles at 2:35 a.m. I don't like walking in a straight line.

I like putting my arm around a stranger because we have the same shirt on and dancing (jumping up and down) to a gay song I don't like. I like arguing about anything with anyone. I like spilling drinks and then buying more. I like to grab onto an exposed pipe and do pull-ups (not chin-ups) because I'm the strongest and bravest guy in the whole world. I like making a 5'4" girl smile when she sees me fearlessly hit the dougie and then putting my hand on the wall behind her so she feels even smaller.

I like falling asleep with my clothes and the lights on. I like waking up on the couch and trying my best to work through the events of last night with my equally useless friends, like a gang of disabled detectives. I like finding clues. I like taking my shirt off because it's too hot and seeing a huge bruise and remembering I told some girl's boyfriend to hit me if he didn't want me talking to her and I gotta hand it to him—he hit me. But how mad can I be? I have a great story to tell and he has a hot girlfriend. We're both winners.

I like mixing vodka with anything that's not vodka. I like mixing weed and tobacco in the galvanized metal socket that is healthy for me to smoke out of. I like to skip breakfast, drink beers, and eat yellow gravity bong hits until I start praying to god for the room to stop spinning. I like to do cocaine in the bathroom stall and spill a lot of it so I can hand the bag back to someone else and act like it was always that full. I like eating something called sassafras and grinding my teeth. (I don't really like grinding my teeth, but you don't have a lot of options when you've got sass in your system).

I like getting fucked up with everyone and everyone likes getting fucked up with me. My favorite person to get fucked up with is Liam. Liam is my roommate and my best friend because a doctor told him he needed to moderate his alcohol intake and he said, "No can do, boss."

Liam knows how to have fun. If an ugly girl starts talking to him, he will hold his breath until she stops. She'll be there talking about class or something while Liam silently nods and turns purple. I have about a hundred videos on my phone of him doing this, and each one is funnier than the last.

One time, this girl would not stop talking and he actually made himself pass out. Crashed right into the bar and took half the shit on it with him. All those lemons and limes. The face that girl made when he connected with the bar top was the lock screen on my phone for a year. My girlfriend (not my girlfriend) said I was gay for making that my lock screen instead of a photo of her, but I've never laughed harder at anything in my life.

That's what it's all about. Having fun. Having a good time. Having some more fun after that. Wake up, get the shakes, and start having fun right away.

That's a joke. I don't actually get the shakes. I'm not an addict, that would be pathetic. I don't *need* to drink or smoke or rail molly. I don't have any trauma I'm trying to forget. Forgetting just makes the remembering more fun. The day getting fucked up stops being fun I'll stop getting fucked up.

Thank God that will never happen.

• • • • •

Like two months ago Liam and I were drinking, playing chel. Only a couple beers in, very recreational stuff, maybe nine on a Tuesday night or something. We're ready to take another gravity bong hit and fully lock into this best of seven series when Liam gets a text.

It's an emergency. This dude Jackson is saying his date bailed on him one drink in, gave him some bullshit about a test she needed to study for. He needs backup so he doesn't look like how he feels.

No problem, the Boys are only a call away. Liam tells him to hold tight and that we'll be there in 15 minutes—a bald-faced lie.

There's just one problem. We're going to the bar and I've only had three beers and one gravity bong hit; I'm practically sober. I try to communicate this problem to Liam, but he's way ahead of me.

"Yeah, there's like—there's no vodka. Or anything. I thought there was like a half a handle in here, but we musta killed it. Or someone took it. I don't know—this is an empty fridge. We don't even have any ketchup or anything."

Uh oh. Jackson's girl trouble is now the last of my worries. I hope I don't kill myself.

I'm kidding (I'm not an addict). I don't actually need to be blacked out before I get to the bar, but man is it more fun that way. Liam picks his controller back up and jokes that Jackson is gonna have to get through this one on his own. I don't have time for jokes so I check his work.

He's right—there's no liquor and we just drank the last seven beers. The Uber is due in five minutes. Five minutes to make a plan and execute.

Three weeks ago, Liam's girlfriend (not his girlfriend) brought this board game over. One of those knock-off "adult" party games. There's a bunch of cards and you're supposed to tell the truth or something when certain cards get pulled—it doesn't matter we never played it. The game came with this bottle of hot sauce, though. Like a really hot one.

It's a small bottle, around the size of a liquor nip, maybe a bit bigger. It's got a warning label on the back though, begging you to take its contents seriously. I throw the hot sauce to Liam and present an airtight argument, "If you don't take a fat pull from that bottle, you're gay."

Liam's smart, but not smart enough to get out this— I've got him in a real bind. I sweeten the deal and tell him if he does it, I'll do it too (I don't know if I'll do it too). He buckles fast.

I've seen some videos online of people eating death sauce, but it's something else in person. There's a brief moment before the flavor takes hold. Where the victim believes they're ok. They're safe. They're stronger than the poison. It's hot, but not that hot.

Those two seconds evaporate and Liam learns that it is **that hot**. He's spitting out of his nose and mouth before the bottle leaves his hand. Sweat pools and he starts breathing with his mouth wide open, panting like a dog. The hot air and rapid breaths only heat up his mouth more. His steaming backdraft hits the back of his throat and triggers a new reaction—now he's gagging and dry-heaving. His coughs are so violent they're more like screams. He might just be screaming, I don't know.

I can tell he's trying to give the bottle back to me and tell me it's my turn, but he's having trouble with words right now. He adds to his pool of spit on the ground and resorts to pointing at the bottle.

I play with the idea of throwing it out the window. Just the thought of airmailing the bottle has me giggling.

Liam's eyes follow mine to the open window and he can't get the words out, but I can tell he's begging me not to do it. Begging me not to fuck him like this.

It would've been funny sure, but I have to honor our arrangement. Something tells me we can't be enemies tonight. Besides, there's a chance it's not even that hot, and he's being a total pussy. I chug the second half of the bottle.

It was that hot. Not much else to say. Liam's no fibber. He wasn't hamming it up. No acting on his part. His nose wasn't growing. No Pinocchios here.

While Liam tries to cram ice cubes in his mouth, I go through my own ritual of understanding. This is how the ant under the magnifying glass must feel. My life has changed for the worse and there's nothing I can do to reverse it. There's no sense in crying about it—all I can do is wait for time or death to take this feeling away.

Liam has his entire mouth around the sink faucet and he's sucking it like a cock. Water spills around his face and up his nose. He's getting quite the facial. Normally I would call him gay, but I have to admit I would love a turn sucking that silver dick.

Liam's phone vibrates—Krist in a silver Kia Nero is here. Time to go.

The bars are only ten minutes away, but I'm present for zero of the ride. When we step out of the car, Liam throws up, as much as he can at least; a beautifully red tie-dyed mixture of beer and bile. It's disgusting, but he looks up at me with the biggest smile—any toxins out of the body seems like a win at this point. I lament the fact that I wasn't able to record it. I love filming people throw up so I can reverse the footage later. It looks like they're eating it that way.

I try to compliment Liam on holding his spew until we got out of the Uber, but nothing comes out. Probably because my shirt is in my mouth and I've been chewing on it for ten minutes. I spit the shirt out and my mouth reignites—I guess that's why I was chewing it. No need to stop now, so I find an un-chewed section and start my second course.

As far as Uber passengers go, we weren't great. Drank both the free waters. Demanded more. Didn't wear seatbelts. Lot of spit out the windows. Liam tried to take his shirt off. I'd guess we earned around a two star trip. Maybe less if Krist noticed how much spit didn't make it out of the windows.

I look up at the bar. O'Malley's. The first of three Irish "pubs" on this block. $4 Bud Lights and Dropkick Murphys in the jukebox. Why the fuck am I even here. Liam pushes past me and gets out his first words, "Where's Jackson."

Oh yeah. I forgot we're here on a charitable mission. Have to cheer this guy up. I don't even know him that well. Only met him a couple times. Way more of Liam's friend. There's a good chance he doesn't even remember my name.

We find Jackson holding down the bar corner, nursing a beer with two empty shot glasses in front of him. I can tell he loves the way he looks with those empty shot glasses. He thinks that's how you're supposed to look when you're sad. I bet the barback tried to clear the glasses and he asked to keep them.

Liam pulls a stool out and sits down next to him. "Yooooo."

He locks in a dap. "Liam, what's up. Thanks for coming." His eyes fall to me. "Yo, what's up man?"

'What's up man?' He definitely doesn't remember my name. That's fine, I'll take the high road. "Good to see you again, *Jackson*."

I pull up the seat next to Liam while he tries to console his buddy. "So, how you doing, man?"

Jackson gestures at the two empty shot glasses. "Pretty good obviously."

I knew it. Two shots and he thinks he's ShoeNice. What a feeling to assume someone is a certain way (non-racistly) and be 100% correct. My night is made. I feel bad he got burned, but later I will be informing Liam that his friend is a ho.

Jackson starts spilling about his date, but I'm fairly tuned out. With Liam sitting in the middle, I was never going to be a contributing member of this conversation. I am surprised to hear Liam talking as much as he is though. My mouth is still raging and I've started chewing on my shirt for the third time. I need a beer.

Maybe throwing up really did relieve some of his pain. Maybe I should try to throw up. Or maybe he never drank half the bottle in the first place. Maybe he took a baby sip, and I drank the whole bottle. That makes sense. I drank way more than him. Of course I did. Fuck me, I need to drink something. I'm running out of fresh shirt.

I'm close to grabbing one of the limes from behind the bar to suck on when I hear a laugh. There's two girls sitting a few seats to my left. Based on their reactions, they've been studying me for a while. Usually I'm pretty aware of my surroundings, but I've been busy chewing fabric for the last five minutes.

They're both cute, which is a rarity. Usually there's a bit of a mismatch in friends. The closer one has dyed blonde hair. The other has shoulder-length black hair. I can't tell if it's dyed. I didn't know girls dyed their hair black until recently. I wonder if they've ever fucked a guy together. I wish I could shut the part of my brain off that thinks this, but that's just the way it is.

Blonde sputters and laughs more publicly after getting caught watching me. Black is a bit more embarrassed and tries to spin Blonde the other way like they were laughing at something else.

Too late now. I feel a bit like an animal in the zoo, but if they want an animal, I'll give them one. I double down on chewing my shirt and look Blonde directly in her eyes.

This cracks them up even more. Blonde raises the question. "Are you good?"

Spthrewww. I spit out my shirt. "I have a condition actually. This is medically prescribed. I'd appreciate it if you were a bit more accepting of the differently abled"

"What's your condition, are you retarded??"

For the first time tonight, I don't think about the burning 10,000 taste buds in my mouth. I can only focus on the burning sensation in my heart. I'm in love.

I crack up, but nobody is laughing harder than Blonde

at her own joke. Black is done trying to reel her in and is focused more on distancing herself from her easily canceled friend. I stand up to join my two new admirers.

Standing up has me confront what I look like. My shirt is fucking disgusting. Soaked and dried and re-soaked with hot sauce spit. The top button is completely missing—I think I bit it off in the car.

I catch a glimpse of myself in the mirror behind the bar. My face is flushed red and my hair is a mess. I look like I ran a 5k to get here. But none of that matters because I have what they really want—a story.

I walk up and introduce myself with the elegance of a man in a $10,000 suit. I give a slight bow and present my hand. Blonde reciprocates and daintily places her hand in mine. I don't kiss it, but I give it a regal lift. This cracks her up even more. I might be the most well-mannered retard she's ever met.

Blonde's name is Alex. I can't remember Black's name. It must not have been important.

Alex raises her drink. "So, actually. Are you good?"

"We watched you chew on your shirt for like, five minutes," adds Black.

She sets me up perfectly. I touch my fingers to my forehead and tilt my profile, giving them my best ironic model pose. " I've been told that women find it difficult to take their eyes off me."

Alex laughs again and it's over. Nuked it. Canon shot. This is batting practice and I'm sending shit to the moon. She doesn't just laugh, but she looks me in the eye when she does it. Only for a moment, then she hides her gaze elsewhere, almost like she's embarrassed of how much she liked it. It's not always this easy, but sometimes it is.

I have three more drinks here in thirty seconds. Bartenders respect you much more when you're with girls and not eating your shirt. I assemble the final piece of the puzzle when I point Liam and Jackson out. Girls need to know you have friends and didn't come alone like a psycho.

With everything taken care of, it's story time now. The Boys join us and we regale the girls with the tale of how we pre-gamed with hot sauce. Two more of Alex's friends show up and Liam spots the roommate of a girl he hooked up with. Our social groups grow and mix and pretty soon we've told this story three or four times. It feels like that scene in *Goodfellas* where everyone knows Henry in the Copa, but on a much smaller pathetic scale.

I kiss Alex during the car ride back. She recoils and I'm worried I blew it, but she lets me know she can still taste the hot sauce in my mouth. I tell her if I eat her out, she might have to go to the hospital.

"And if I swallow you I'll have to get my stomach pumped."

Our kids can never hear this story.

I text Alex two days later to try and meet up, but she doesn't respond.

Normally I'd never double text. I can take a hint, but this hint I don't want to take. I send her a screenshot of the hot sauce in my Amazon cart followed by, "round 2??

TongueEmoji FireEmoji."

What the fuck is wrong with me. Before my thumb slips off send, I've already thrown my phone into my bed. I'm so disgusted I do 100 push-ups to cleanse my soul. Our meeting felt like magic, but in my post-fitness clarity I can examine the night more forensically. She was drunk, and I was what she wanted at the time.

At the time.

That's fine. That's ok. We both got something out of it.

I'm a little annoyed that it feels like she got more out of it than me though. I'm a competitor at heart. If I run into her again I might call her the wrong name, eke out a win that way. Alexa? Or something foreign like Izzy? What's crueler, a syllable off like I remember her, but not clearly, or a completely different name, like I'm mixing her up with another girl? Or no name at all? Just let it hang until she has to say it herself?

What the fuck is wrong with me. Planning how I'm going to misremember someone's name? No one who ever fought in the coliseum has had a thought like this. Girl-brain is infecting my psyche. A full purge is necessary.

I put on *Goodfellas* and do another 100 push-ups. That's better. I'm nothing like the man I was ten minutes ago. I'm like all of these guys.

If we meet up again, whatever happens happens. The only people who dwell on interactions this long are losers and women. She wasn't even that hot. I hope I run into her again and she sees me doing something cool, like dunking or getting arrested.

• • • • •

"I said the joker is a wanted man, he makes his way all across the land."

Joker and the Thief plays in the NHL menu. I must've heard it twice by now. Liam's been in the bathroom for way too long. A double digit loss usually creates a need for reflection, but it's been fifteen minutes. This is too much reflection.

He comes out and picks his controller back up. "Let's go, run it back."

"You gonna sit down?" Liam is standing in front of the screen like how dads watch TV.

"Yeah, in a bit. I got a hot ass right now, gotta stand for a minute."

"You need medicine. Ointments. Some kind of balm."

"And I bet you'd love to put it on me. Start it up."

"That shit was two days ago. Something is wrong with you if you're still shitting fire."

"I don't know what to tell you. For some reason my body was not ready to process half a bottle of hot sauce that came with a warning label."

I still don't think he drank half the bottle, but he's not lying about his bodily failures. Spending any time with Liam over the last two days has to come in intervals because half the time he's in the bathroom. This is his second break of the session.

Still standing, Liam rips X to randomize his teams. Oilers. Penguins. "I don't need a third, gimme the Pens."

335

"Whatever it takes." I'll be going to war with the Wild, a much more honorable team.

First period and Liam doesn't hesitate to implement psychological warfare. "That girl text you back yet?"

I should never have told him how bad I folded. "Yeah, I'm getting the feeling she's busy tonight."

"Maybe tomorrow then. I'm sure she'll be free tomorrow."

"We were gonna hang tomorrow, but she's actually fucking a bunch of guys that night. Running through the whole football team. The day after she said she might be able to squeeze me in."

"Oh great, I'm happy for you. Really seemed like you two had a connection."

"Thanks, I thought so too."

Crosby's on a breakaway. He's too fast, one on one with the goalie. Liam can't deke for shit so he just winds up a slap shot prayer. He cocks the stick back and lets it rip—pipe city. The puck bounces off the right post and finds its way in. Goal.

"LET'S GO!"

Fuck. It doesn't feel good going down early, but I can't be that mad about a luckbox goal. I grab Liam's shirt and pull him down, forcing contact between his torched asshole and the couch.

"Shit, come on man, I'm on IR."

"Yeah, irregular... uhh..." I can't think of a word for shitting that starts with R.

Liam encourages me. "You're almost there, you got it."

"...Retardation."

"Incredible."

I gotta focus. End the period strong. Liam's relaxed, already counting this as a win. One goal after the beating he just took, it must feel like one.

After the first period I'm up 2-1. We agree on a timeout to take another gravity bong hit. The machine needs fuel.

Liam's GB hits his throat harsh and sends him into a coughing fit. He settles after a minute or two and stares at the wall, deep in thought. "That was fun though, right?"

"What?"

"Last night, the bar. The hot sauce shit."

"That was two nights ago."

"Whatever, you know what I'm talking about."

I do know what he was talking about, but it's fun to be right. "Yeah, definitely. One for the books."

"We should do it again."

"You've been shitting steam for two days. I think medically I would have to intervene."

"Not hot sauce, fuck that. I'm never drinking that shit again. But something like that for sure." Liam adjusts his shorts and leans further back on the couch so he's sitting more on his back instead of his ass. I clock it all, but say nothing.

"What is like hot sauce? You want to start eating ghost peppers before we go out?"

"That's not what I'm saying, forget the hot shit. How many times have we gotten hammered before we go out?"

I want to interject and tell him "every time," but it

seems like he actually has a thought he's trying to articulate.

Liam continues his lecture. "How many times have
we hit the grav or crushed up Vyvanse? There's a bit of a
routine, right? Don't get me wrong, it's still fun, but that
night we tapped into something new. Like. Remember
how exciting drinking was before you were 21? When getting a bottle was something that took a week of planning?
Or what smoking felt like before you did it every day? I'd
send out five messages trying to find someone who would
sell an eighth for less than 60 bucks. Then you're meeting
dude in a park trying to look normal while you hand him
the most mismatched 50 dollars you've ever held. I'd be
buying weed with a 20, three 5s, eleven 1s, and then like,
quarters. I once bought weed from Rachel's boyfriend
with six dollars in quarters. He looked at me like, 'Really, dude?' But he took the quarters man. Wow. Probably
for laundry. What was I saying? I have no idea what I'm
talking about shit my head is buzzing. Feel like I got a
helmet on."

I have no idea what he's talking about either—all of
my energy is on the ice. It's 4-1 me.

• • • • •

Read four days ago.

Alex isn't texting me back and that's fine. For a moment I wonder if I should text her something like a super
zoomed in photo of Pablo Prigioni to show her I don't

care. Funny, but no. Any performative act of not caring is caring. The only way to not care is not to care.

Out of last night's grav bong stupor, I'm seeing things more clearly. Liam got so high he tried to order a pizza with his driver's license. Took him three tries before he realized he wasn't punching in the numbers on his debit card. An all-time high guy move, but in the aftermath I'm beginning to understand what he was trying to say.

When I was in high school there was this kid, Oliver. Completely standard issue student. Social, but not popular. JV Soccer, but never varsity. He went to prom, but took a girl from a different school. Nothing against him, but he was a lead candidate to take up space in a yearbook and never anyone's memories.

Except for junior year after winter break.

You see your guys over break, but I was never venturing that far out of the core circle, so when you get back, there's a bit of a class reunion. You check in with the people you haven't seen. See what's changed (nothing), what they've been up to (nothing).

I remember talking with Mason, the guy I sit next to in Spanish, but never hang out with outside of school. He went skiing with his family, but he actually tried snowboarding this time. Wow.

People are shooting the shit, catching up, and then Oliver walks in with his arm in a sling and a black eye. He looks like he got the shit beat out of him, but he's not carrying himself like that. He looks proud. Probably prouder than he's ever looked walking into school.

His presence immediately supersedes whatever bullshit story Mason is telling. Oliver doesn't announce anything, but a signal goes up that he's the only one with something worth listening to. Pretty soon he's entertaining the biggest audience he's ever had.

Four days ago, Oliver was in the city with his sister and his mom. They're shopping or some shit, Mom's taking forever, so Oliver and his sister wait outside.

They end up walking a few stores down the block when some insane dude appears. His clothes are ripped, no shoes, screaming at everybody on the street. The type of guy you just hope ignores you. He might've been homeless, mentally ill, dangerous, who knows. The only thing Oliver knew for sure was that he was angry.

This guy gets in Oliver's face and starts asking for change, but he's not really asking for change you know? He just wants to dominate. Before Oliver can even say, "no," this guy is asking again. Getting way too close to him. Closing the distance. Taking up Oliver's space. Saying shit like, "I know you got money man, look at your little girlfriend here. I know you buy her shit."

Oliver said he could feel himself freezing up. A combination of fight/flight response and being accused of dating his sister had him all flustered. He really dragged this part out in his story, let us all know how terrified he was, but he knew he had to protect his sister. I'll give him some credit, he definitely knew how to sell this story to the girls in the audience.

He doesn't know what to do. This guy is acting crazy, but he hasn't actually done anything yet. You can't just hit a guy for talking to you, right? But you don't want to run and make something out of nothing. Oliver tries to get his sister to start walking backwards, but she's even more scared than he is.

His sister is too scared to move. She's actually frozen. The dude keeps pressing them, turning more attention to his sister. Oliver is grabbing her arm, but she's not budging.

Her feet are rooted to the sidewalk, but she manages to send a brain signal to her arm to pull her phone out. I don't know if she was calling her mom or the police, but she raises her phone to her head to involve another party.

The psycho doesn't want her phoning a friend. He puts his palm to her hand and pushes right through her head. Sends her straight to the ground and her phone goes flying.

That's it. Contact is an invitation. Some guys go their whole lives waiting for a justifiable fight like this. Free reign to reenact every UFC fight you've ever watched. The only way this could be better is if his sister actually was his girlfriend.

Go time. Oliver tackles him and starts giving him ground and pound. He gets in some sloppy shots, but quickly finds out the UFC is much harder than it looks from the couch. They roll around, trade hits, Oliver gets his eye blacked, then some good samaritan pulls him up. Oliver wins by decision.

Oliver stands over his opponent and tells him, "Don't ever fuck with my sister again." At this point, I'm starting to wonder how much of the story is getting re-edited in front of me. I believe Oliver said some shit after the fight, but I think it was more likely heavy breathing and something disjointed, like, "Don't... ever...you fuck with us..."

What a story though, and it was told even better. People were so wrapped up in the electricity nobody even asked him about his arm. I guess people just assumed it was from the scrap, same way he got the black eye. I found out two weeks later from another guy on the soccer team that Oliver fractured his arm, but it wasn't from the fight.

This part didn't make it into the story, but after he delivered his victory speech, the homeless dude popped back up for round two. Oliver didn't sign up for more rounds so he grabs his sister and they book it. They sprint the block and make their getaway, but not before Oliver runs straight into a mailbox.

Too fucking funny. Kid beats up a homeless guy, then runs away and breaks his own arm. I kept his secret for as long as I could (one and a half weeks).

Regardless of how he told it, the general story was all true. Oliver stood up for his sister and no one can take that away from him. He won winter break and got to enjoy legend status for a good week and a half. Don't think I ever saw him doing anything in study hall except for studying, and that day I saw him talking to a senior cheerleader. He even tried out wearing his hat backwards and tongue fucking his shoes. Crazy what fame will do to you.

So why am I reminiscing on Oliver's title fight? It was a funny story and I love to tell it to people, but I'm starting to see we've got more in common than I thought.

Both of us took a spectacle and capitalized on it. One

little story turned a regular appearance into something extraordinary. Something the crowd around us couldn't ignore.

It's not much of a realization now that I realize it. People who have done things are more interesting than people who haven't. Wow. Genius. I should write that down so I don't forget it.

This is what Liam was trying to articulate, though. When you first start drinking it feels special. A brand new activity that makes you stand out from everyone else. Especially from those who aren't doing it. Showing up to prom as a part of the chosen few to have had three whole beers is enough to make you look like Hugh Heffner. A couple years and a thousand beers later, drinking has lost of a bit of its luster.

So if we need something beyond drinking, what? I think we're off hot sauce and I don't see me or Liam fighting the homeless any time soon.

What's the next pre-game?

• • • • •

A cowboy shot is when you rip a bong, take a shot, and then exhale. Bongs are expensive and breakable (we've broken too many) so we opt for the more industrious plastic gravity bong. Our current setup involves a 32oz Gatorade bottle floating in an Utz pretzel tub. It takes a strong man to hit cowboys out the grav, but that's what we are. Strong men.

When Liam does cowboys though he'll forego the weed and stuff the bowl with tobacco. Then he sprinkles kief on top of that. We call this a "sitter" because the head rush of grav bonging tobacco is so intense it's impossible to stand up afterwards. The namesake comes into play and sitting down becomes your only option.

I'll do a sitter every now and then to show I can, but it's a part of Liam's regular diet. We started doing them when we were out of weed, but now Liam will do it even when the jar is full. It disgusts me to no end that he regularly smokes tobacco out of a bong and still has better cardio than me.

There's a Barack Obama shot glass filled with tequila next to the grav rig. Liam throws it back and releases the yellow smoke from his lungs. He lets out a few controlled coughs and sinks back into the couch. Obama seems to approve. *Yes We Can.*

It takes a good 30-45 seconds to be released from the effects of a sitter. No point in talking to him now, he won't be able to answer. Deep in thought, he grips the Xbox controller and scrolls through the menus. He has no destination, but it feels good to control something.

On the dot, 46 seconds later, Liam emerges from his meditation and hits me with the plan. Still staring straight ahead, still flicking between the menus. "We should fight."

"What?"

"We should fight each other before the party. So when we get there we look fucked up and shit."

It's not the worst idea he's ever had. It's fucking stupid, but I've had a few drinks myself so we might as well take

344

the hypothetical for a walk. Time for Socratic dialogue.

"You think that's gonna set tonight off? If we show up bloodied to Chelsea's birthday?"

"Yeah, pretty much. Just like the hot sauce. We'll pull up scrapped and say we got jumped or something. We can say we fought off like six townies. Be a crazy story. Everybody's gonna love it."

"A crazy story we made up."

"You're stressing over details. The fight will be real, that's what matters."

I'll admit it, I don't want to fight Liam. He's bigger than me, stronger than me, and probably a better fighter than me. I don't think he wants to fight me either, but he's for sure the favorite.

Not that he'd win every time, though. If we simulated our brawl 100 times, I have to believe I take at least 10-20 of them. There are some realities where he trips and I get in ten clean 12-6 elbows. You gotta believe in yourself.

Seven beers has me curious though. We haven't talked about it until now, but we've both been thirsting after another pre-game stunt. If this was reversed and Liam was six inches shorter than me, I would be moving the couch and making an octagon right now.

I don't mind the destination, but the vehicle isn't working for me. "Dude, I'm not fighting you."

"You scared?"

"Scared for you. I watched ten minutes of *The Karate Kid* last night. The new one where the kid's black. I've got a fresh arsenal filled with forbidden techniques."

Liam laughs, but he presses me further. "Come on. I'm not saying we fight to the death. We don't even fight for real. We just trade. You punch me, I punch you. Easy."

"There's no way you're getting the speed right. Let me tell you how it's gonna go. First shot, you tap me too soft to bruise, next shot you try to go harder, but still tap me soft again, third try you unload and I wake up on the floor."

"That sounds fine to me, let's get it."

I've gotta throw some evidence at him before I end up hospitalized. "A black eye isn't even gonna show up today. We hit each other now and the bruise won't be visible until tomorrow." I have no idea if this is true, but it sounds like it could be.

"Ok, so what then?"

My eyes scan the room for help. What instrument in the apartment can hurt me without hurting me? I don't need a lot, just enough to break the ice.

In between controllers, empty red cups, and the grav, there's a cutting board covered with the remnants of a frozen pizza. Nestled under crusts, there's the 5-inch knife we used to cut it in half.

Liam catches me staring at the blade. "No way. You were too pussy to take a punch. That's actually insane."

It is insane, but it's starting to click for me. I pick up the knife and run it through a paper towel to clean off the tomato sauce. "This is something we can control. You try to throw a punch and who knows how strong it's coming out? This is surgical. Just a nick and we're good to go."

Liam's mouth is open. He's stunned, but he hasn't

said no yet. I'm sure a minute ago he was positive he was the dumbest guy in the room. Not a chance while I'm here.

"Where then?"

"Where what?"

"Where do we do it?"

Holy shit, he's game. "I don't know. Hand? That way it's visible. Almost like jewelry."

"Hand? Like my palm? I'm not doing that, it's gonna fuck up my spiral."

"Your spiral? You're not going to the fucking league, man."

"Yeah, definitely not if you cut my fucking hand."

Somehow after I suggested that we cut each other, he's still the most deluded guy here.

He continues. "If I wake up tomorrow and I can't throw a perfect spiral I would just kill myself." Liam's got principles. I can't deny that.

"Ok, not the hand... what about face? Like above the eye. Forehead zone."

I've got his attention with this one. "That is a cool place for a cut. Very classy. I like it."

I've cleared all the pizza slime off the knife now. Good as new. Ready for operation. If I had been drinking less today, I might've had a thought about sanitization, but that's an irrelevant "if."

I present the handle to Liam. "Who first? You want to do me or other way around?"

Liam takes the knife and feels the weight. He tries some different grips, blade up, blade down, feeling out the proper technique.

"You know, you might be right about putting too much weight behind the punch. I'm not gonna feel great if I hit the cut too hard and slice through to your skull. If we do this, we should do ourselves."

That seems logical, but why hadn't I thought of that? There's something pathetically emo about cutting yourself. If we're gonna do this, I wanted to at least do it in a cool way.

He has a point about control though. Liam's intake has been steady tonight and he has a habit of breaking glasses by dropping them. No need for him to be in charge of my surgery. He hands the knife back to me.

I examine the tool one last time. The knife is light. Sharp enough too. I use my left hand to spread the skin above my eye. Feeling out where to make the incision.

This is the first time I've asked for this without coke. I look back at Liam. "Get the mirror."[1]

---

1 When you're writing about something you're familiar with, it can feel like a flow state. At least for me, it feels more like listening than writing. It's how I imagine a stenographer feels. There's no thinking to be had, just recording what is already there. I don't have to make a decision about what's being said or how it's being said, because I'm not even aware of those decisions. I'm recording a history and there's no room for editing what is written in stone.

The blocks come when you try to write about something you don't understand. A fight written by someone who has never thrown a punch. A breakup written by someone who's never been in love. Hunger from someone has never starved. It all feels so hollow.

I believe you can get close. You mix a little bit of your truths in with the fiction and something halfway believable comes out. A great writer can do that and make imagination feel like a diary. That's not me though. I need the primary source cheat code. It makes it so much easier.

This is where I got stuck. I started writing a story about a guy who likes to get fucked up. He likes the social butter of substance abuse, but starts replacing it with more dangerous activities like drinking hot sauce and eventually self-harm. Imagine pre-gaming for a bar by cutting a finger off just so you have something to talk to girls about. Hahahaha, very funny, you get it.

The beginning was easy. I've drank before. I've smoked before. I've eaten things that were given to me and thrown them up later. I know those feelings and it felt easy to weave a story around them. Like it usually does for me, it felt like listening. As the story went on it though, I hit a wall.

I get to the point where I need this character to cut himself and I'm having trouble with it. Because I have a normal brain (something I will be proving false shortly) I have never dabbled in self-harm. I try to write around it, but everything I put down doesn't feel as real as what I started with. It doesn't mesh. Doesn't connect. I don't have the primary sources I normally draw from.

My brief experience is a foggy middle school memory. Huddled together with a few friends in the hallway before it was spilled: "Alice cuts. She told me. I saw her legs."

At the time, I was dumbfounded. My legs were perpetually cut from playing football every day. Why would someone do that on purpose? At least I was getting touchdowns. Is she a moron?

My brain has not developed much since then, as I clearly don't understand self-harm any better. So what do you do when you're stuck? Learn.

Who cuts?
Why do they cut?
What does it feel like when they cut?
Does it feel satisfying or embarrassing?
Is it always with a knife?
Do they burn themselves or use other tools?
What does it take to start and what does it take to stop?
Answers to all this and more on Reddit dot com.

Reddit can be a great source to learn about a new topic, but you have to remember you're learning about it from people who want to discuss it on Reddit. With this caveat in mind, I scroll for around twenty minutes, leaving slightly more educated than I was twenty minutes ago.

Most people exhibit self-destructive behavior at a young age that leads to cutting later. It frequently starts with biting, scratching, hair pulling, and then develops into burning or cutting. The majority start within the ages of 11-15, with "gateway" behavior even earlier.

Some people do it to assert control in their life. Some do it to punish themselves. Some admit they did it because they were bored. Most, if not all, regret it later in life. It's more of an addiction than I originally thought. Many still deal with relapses up into their early 20s.

This is a good baseline, but nothing that feels helpful to my story. I briefly feel something reading a post where a mother begs for help after walking in on her daughter pushing a knife into her arm. Hundreds of replies flood in, telling her not to invade her daughter's privacy as it will only push them further into SH (self-harm), obviously coming from first-hand experience.

The mom wonders if it's her fault. Everyone assures her it's not, but I just read ten posts where people blame their parents for their start in self-harm. What am I doing.

Should I be mining the worst day of this woman's life for specks of truth?

I do some self-reflecting of my own. Will this really make me a better writer?

Obviously, yes. Of course it will. I'm like Hunter S. Thompson. An author I have never read before and have no familiarity with beyond the vague idea that he was a guy who really got up in there. That's what I'm doing. Getting up in there.

I return to the forum and refine my search with the keyword "attention." This reasoning is more in line with my character and there are plenty of posts about it. People don't love the word "attention," but liken it more to a "cry for help." Posters acknowledge that it's quite common for people to self-harm to get people to notice them. Those that feel ignored or left behind take a drastic action to get the attention they feel they're missing. Like sending out an SOS.

Slightly different from my story about a bro cutting before hitting the bar, but not that different. I can work with this. I feel more confident writing now that my idea has some reflection in reality. I salute the brave posters of r/SelfHarm and take my leave.

Now I can write my story.

Now I can write my story, so why am I not writing it? Another week drifts by and my new self-harm knowledge has done nothing to push my hand. Still stuck. Blocked. Struggling to make it feel real.

I sculpt out a paragraph about cutting and it explodes in the kiln. No structure, it wasn't built to last. Delete, delete, delete.

I bounce between the forums and my blank page. If I read enough of these depressive diaries, I'll find something that sparks an idea. I have to. I just haven't found it yet.

Somewhere in the middle of a post about how a girl is worried she isn't cutting deep enough for her self-harm to count (the community assures her it does count) I decide I need a break. A step away to clear my head. No sense forcing the words when they're not there. They'll come when they come, I'm in no rush.

Another week floats by and I get a splinter at work. Deep dead center of my left thumb. Maybe a half inch long and completely submerged in skin. I'm supposed to go bowling later and I'm worried about how this will affect my game.

Normally I'd use a tweezer and try to get in there, but there's nothing to grab on to. The entirety of the splinter is inside my hand. I dive back online for some research and learn that using a sterilized needle can help push the splinter to the surface. I've never done much sewing, so I don't have a needle. I dig through the rest of my shit and find the closest analogue, my pocket knife.

A good citizen online pitches in and says a knife will do in a pinch if you don't have a needle. If someone writes it online, it can't be that bad of an idea. I position myself in the bathroom under surgical lights and start the operation.

It's hard to cut yourself. I have a newfound respect for the authors of every post

I read. I can't manage a baby laceration and there are people out there literally addicted to it.

I bounce the knife off my thumb dozens of times without breaking skin at all. I tell myself it's a dull blade, but truly there's some recess of my mind that knows I'm not supposed to do this. That sounds much better than admitting I'm a pussy.

Ten minutes go by and I've barely managed to chip away at a micrometer of the splinter. This hobby is not for me. Dejected, I put my knife away and accept I'll have to wait a week until my body spits the foreign object back out.

I go bowling and it kind of hurts my hand to hold the ball. I put up 148 and crush all my co-workers.

Another week passes. Probably more, but I've stopped counting. I'm no closer to the story I want to write and truthfully it feels like I'm drifting further away from it. Still nothing worthwhile and all I want is to be finished with this book. I need a deadline. If I can't finish this one, I might just trash it.

One last attempt before I put her down. Instead of my usual style of sitting at the computer and hoping something good comes out I try to actually analyze what's not working.

I have a problem with authenticity. Everything written needs to feel like it happened and right now there's no page I write that would stand up to scrutiny from the 100,000+ members of the self-harm subreddit. One sentence and they'd know I was a fraud. Writing from the outside.

I feel the same way when I see someone take acid in a movie and start to hallucinate pink elephants. Why are you putting this in the movie when you've clearly never taken acid? The only thing that's gonna happen when you take psyches is you laugh for 90 minutes and look at trees. So obviously fake. Not only does the end product suck, but you expose yourself as an imposter. An even worse crime.

What I want is something that has to be experienced. The research will get you to the edge, but you can't know what it feels like to fall until you jump. What I've learned isn't enough. It's not getting me close to the purity I need.

Unfortunately I know now what will.

You always see people in movies sterilizing knives by holding them over a fire. My medical experience is limited so this seems like a good starting point. I've got rubbing alcohol pads too, those should help. Fire before alcohol? But then the blade will be too hot to touch with the pads. I guess the knife doesn't need to be burning hot during. So hold the blade in the fire, wait for it to cool down, and then coat it with the alcohol.

I briefly consider googling "how to safely self-harm," but that feels like the only thing more embarrassing than what I'm about to do. Even in incognito mode with history and cookies deleted one hundred times over, I can't do it. I can't face God with that in my life's search history. That's a history that can't be erased.

My knife is so dull too. Fried from years of cutting through boxes, tape and zip ties at work. I've got a second fresher knife that was a gift from an ex, but that seems like an even sadder tool to damage myself with.

I can't imagine using a knife from the kitchen either. No way am I gonna be chopping onions with the same blade I sinned with. I can't do that. Buying a new knife just for this seems awfully sad too. I'm realizing there are very few ways to do this honorably.

I saw a 3-pack of paring knives at the grocery store the other day for $6. I could give two to the kitchen, use the third, and then just throw it out after. But what if one of my roommates goes to the grocery store and sees those same knives for sale in a 3-pack? Would they ask where the third knife is? Could they put it together?

I do a couple of tests on an orange peel and decide my Leatherman will have to do. It pierces the peel which is good enough for me. The orange tastes good too, which is a nice distraction from my developing mental illness.

Location, location, location. Where? Has to be the thigh. It's concealed and has the most amount of fat, something I'm fairly short on. I'm moderately concerned about piercing the femoral artery, which I believe is something important in the leg. I'm already committed to an activity this stupid though, so there's no way that will stop me. I mentally mark it, *Don't hit the femoral artery*, even though I have no idea where or what it is.

Every step of the way where I might falter, I remind myself that teenage girls do this all the time. If they can do it, I can do it. There is no activity a 13-year-old girl can do that I can't. It's inspirational and I need as much inspiration as I can get.

With my shorts rolled up to my balls, I look down at my leg. Two months ago I walked through a lake and cut my ankle on a shell. It's still healing. I notice the cut every time I put socks on. As a kid, I flayed my knee open with a nasty rug burn while playing tag. Then I re-opened that same cut three times over playing football. Over 15 years later, and there's still a scar on my knee. The human body remembers so much. I hope it can forget this.

Should I really do this? It would be soft to stop now. I can feel my heroes watching over me, cheering me on. Every wrestler who bladed. Every film's action hero who cut a bullet out. Every girl who had a Tumblr account. I can't let them down.

What do we sacrifice for art? Can sacrifice alone be enough to make art? David Blaine starved himself on webcam in a plexiglass box for 44 days, drinking only 4.5L of water a day. Chris Burden's most famous work is a short film where he stands against a wall and has his friend shoot him in the arm with a rifle. Van Gogh cut his fucking ear off and gave it to a prostitute. I've never been that horny in my life, but still. You have to admire his drive.

I am just like those guys. Pushing my body to the limit to retrieve something extraordinary from the other side. It's brave what I'm doing. What I'm doing is brave. I am being brave. I am brave.

Pain is different when you watch it happen. When you control it. When you're ready to receive it. I would guess most people's experience with pain is accidental. I know mine is. A slip, a crash, a spill. Once it happens, it's already over. Your finger's jammed, your shin's bruised, your arm's broken. You might not even feel it at first. Your brain is always looking out for you. What you don't know can't hurt you.

Looking at unharmed flesh and making the decision to change it is something else. I hate to recommend it and I don't, but there's something to it. Nothing good, but something.

There's a wall you have to break through. The same wall I struggled against when I tried to cut the splinter out. For me, seven beers was the recipe to knock it down.

Next is a feeling of extremity. The ultimate distraction. I can see how this could feel like a cure to someone whose mind is so clouded. I don't mean to be so literal, but it cuts right through it.

You may disagree with my assessment, but at the time, I had a clear mind. With no mental pain to cut through, I faced the actual pain far too fast.

Stopstopstopstopwhatareyoudoing. I have to stop.

At this point, I felt all the other walls behind the first. What it would take to go longer. Go deeper. Go again.

I hold a bandage to my leg, trying to focus on the pressure of my hand rather than the feeling underneath it. I can't even look at it. Seven beers is not enough for this. There's no number that's enough for this.

Time for art. Can I finish the story now? Have I learned enough?

Dragging a knife through two inches of my leg leads me to realize nothing meaningful about the condition of self-harmers. I realize nothing about art. What I do realize is that I'm a fucking idiot.

I revisit my earlier inspiration. What do we sacrifice for art? Can the sacrifice alone be enough?

I have the answer now. Who gives a fuck. Maybe for other dumber people, but for me, no. Not at all. Not even close. My leg hurts. Bad. Why did I do that. If anyone sees my thigh I'm gonna have to make up some shit about a cactus.

I don't care about the rest of this story any more.

www.ingramcontent.com/pod-product-compliance
Lightning Source LLC
Chambersburg PA
CBHW020820180626
46814CB00001B/41